# UNDEVELOPED LOVE

## BOOK 5

## VIRGINIA'DELE SMITH

**BOOKS ARE UBIQUITOUS**

Published by Books are Ubiquitous, Inc.
in the United States of America
booksareubiquitous.com

*Books are Ubiquitous* is a federally registered trademark.

This book is a work of fiction.

Names, characters, places, and incidents either are the product of the author's imagination or are used fictitiously. Any resemblance to actual persons, living or dead, business establishments, events, or locales is entirely coincidental.

ISBN: 978-1-957036-09-0

———

## Titles by Virginia'dele Smith

*For my mom, Vickie…MawMaw*

*Thank you for instilling in me
your joyful cheer for all things Christmas,
your passion for creating beautiful
spaces and celebrations,
and your devout gift of focusing on
and loving our family.*

*But to you who are listening I say:*
*Love your enemies,*
*do good to those who hate you...*
*Luke 6:27*

*Thursday, December 10, 2020*

Two oak trees, full and green and immense in their girth, loomed over the entrance to Twin Oaks. They towered above the driveway and guarded the gate like fierce defenders. Blake Fisher squinted at one trunk and then at the other. Just as she'd suspected, angry faces appeared in the thick, rough bark. Those trees had stood watch over the Sharps' ranch for a hundred and forty years; they knew as well as Blake did exactly who belonged there — and who did not.

A work truck exited the property, providing Blake the opportunity she needed. She scooted her old but dependable FJ Cruiser through the entrance — without permission. Her impeccable timing was not a coincidence. She'd cased the ranch, tracked the comings and goings of the cowboys, staff, and family members who lived there. Her reconnaissance had paid off. Hypothetically, Blake had scaled the walls of Camelot.

She pushed aside a twinge of guilt, pretending it was a sense of accomplishment that caused the flutter in her stomach. And really, the trespassing couldn't be helped. After months of returned letters, ignored emails, and rejected calls, the Sharps had forced Blake to take matters into her own hands.

*So this is Twin Oaks.*

Begrudgingly, Blake admitted — if only to herself — that descriptions and photos didn't do it justice.

She drove under a dense canopy of spindly bare branches attached to more ancient oaks that lined the brick drive. Beyond the perfectly placed trees, pipe fencing created a perimeter around rolling pastures thick with winter rye, frolicking horses, and more giant trees. The metal of the posts, painted a pristine white and radiant with the sun's bright light, projected an air of cool, clean, crisp, and stately magnificence.

The Big House, as they called it, hadn't come into view yet, but if the landscape looked snobby and off-putting, the house would be even worse. Heaven knew the family inside made stuck-up look downright gracious.

Two curves and a bridge later, Blake topped a hill and came face-to-face with all Twin Oaks's fabled and illustrious glory. Her foot lifted from the gas pedal as her mind processed the incredible view ahead. A strong and exquisite ranch house, constructed with a perfect blend of logs, planks, rocks, and bricks, sat prominently in the middle of a brilliant clearing. That many shades of brown with such a mixture of materials should have looked disjointed. Instead, the sprawling structure looked as though it had been born of the earth on which it stood. Mimicking the impressive fence line, white shutters reflected the sun and brought the landscaping and the lodging together. An array of colorful cold-weather flowers, bright red winterberry shrubs, and ornamental foliage decorated pots and planters on the front porch. More of the same filled beds edged in low strips of aged and weathered metal, and even more foliage trailed onto the grounds, seamlessly separating the house from the fields.

Neither cold nor foreboding, Twin Oaks appeared cheerful and welcoming.

Blake knew better.

————

"*W*hy is that rust bucket out front?" Hudson Sharp ignored his brother's question.

"Who's the babe stepping out of it?"

Hudson Sharp ignored his *other* brother's question.

"And where has she been all my life?"

Hudson Sharp ignored his *third* brother's question.

He'd learned long ago that his best chance of finding peace and quiet came with simply *not* answering. Speaking to the boys invited more conversation, which created more noise, which Hudson abhorred. Taken one at a time, the triplets wore Hudson out; together, they functioned like a tsunami-tornado in the middle of a tropical storm…best to hunker down and hide until they passed through.

As hoped and expected, they wandered off when he declined to engage.

Less humored by their antics than their doting parents, Hudson wanted the nineteen-year-olds to develop a desire for something beyond girls, friends, and good times. After their freshman year of rodeoing for Tarleton State University, their grades were fine, but not great. They had done well enough to earn newcomer-of-the-year honors that season, but they had to improve if they wanted to make it to the College National Finals Rodeo.

As their older brother, Hudson had somehow assumed responsibility for their futures when he'd accepted responsibility for running the ranch. In one fell swoop, their mom and dad had announced that with the triplets gone to college, it was past time for them to start "experiencing life." They'd named Hudson president and managing member of their family corporation, bought a seventy-five-foot superyacht, and set out to spend their retirement on the water until someone gave them a good reason to come home, namely grandbabies to spoil. They had made no mention of leaving their three young hellions in Hudson's charge. But someone had to keep an eye on them, and with no other volunteers vying for the role, it had fallen to Hudson to be their guardian.

In the eleven months since that big revelation last Christmas, a global pandemic had sent the boys home full-time, forcing them to take their college classes over the internet. With an endless supply of energy, a low tolerance for boredom, and one another to encourage poor decisions, the triplets were quite a handful. By Hudson's accounting, the boys were more difficult to manage than their sixty-seven-thousand-acre cattle ranch. And a horse farm. And a hobby-level goat dairy that produced milk, cheese, and soaps. And a patch of Christmas trees.

Hudson couldn't forget the Christmas trees...the current bane of his existence — outside his siblings, of course.

Years ago, before his Loony Aunt Juni — her chosen moniker, not of Hudson's doing — traded in her layered skirts and bohemian scarves for haute couture and thousand-dollar stilettos, Juniper Roxanne Sharp had scattered thirty handfuls of fir, pine, spruce, and cypress seedlings across thirty acres on the southeast boundary of the ranch to commemorate her thirtieth birthday. She'd put no thought into the planting, hadn't spaced the seeds, and had paid zero attention to irrigation. As a result of her haphazard behavior — and indicative of

Juniper's Midas touch — Twin Oaks housed one of the most bountiful Christmas tree farms in Oklahoma.

Hudson allowed the trees to be harvested only because if he did not thin them out per a specific soil management schedule, the acreage would suffer. He refused to sell them; instead, Hudson had worked a deal with their preacher, Mr. Mitchell, to set up a tree lot at the church. It opened the day after Thanksgiving and closed on Christmas Eve. The youth group worked the lot every year, and in exchange, the kids kept everything they earned to fund summer camps and mission trips. Best of all, Hudson kept his name completely out of the deal.

He might also have allowed the harvesting because the trees remained important to Aunt Juni, but he'd never admit such a thing in her presence. As CEO of Juniper Goat Co., a division of Sharp Enterprises, she oversaw the goat dairy. The world believed she'd abandoned her free-spirited ways, settled down in Green Hills, and burned her bangles and coin skirts. But underneath her Harvard business degree, her fierce boardroom negotiations, and her incredible knack for marketing campaigns, his beloved Loony Aunt Juni still shared his obsession for the land, the scent of the evergreens, the neighing of horses and mooing of cows, and the pull of the soil. She still walked barefoot through the fields, dabbled in floral oils and fragrance creations for soaps and candles, and swam in the pond. Above all else, she adored Christmas.

Hudson could no more allow harm to come to those thirty acres than he could stab himself in the heart.

Which explained why he'd avoided Blake Fisher, the real estate agent blowing up his phone, his email, and his DMs on social media, like the plague. Seriously, who stalked a man over direct message, anyway?

———

*B*lake eased her Santa-suit-red SUV the rest of the way up the brick drive, soaking up as many details as possible…just in case they tossed her off the premises and banned her from returning after her first visit.

The landscape and the house were just the beginning. Multiple barns, numerous outbuildings, a chicken coop far larger than her home and office, an elegant greenhouse, and the most delightful wraparound porch Blake had ever seen accented the property with color and warmth. Everywhere she looked, something looked lovely.

Blake parked her vehicle, walked to the porch of the Big House, and stepped up to the tall double doors. Taking a deep breath to settle and steel her nerves, Blake lifted her hand to knock. Before her knuckles rapped on the intricately carved wood, one of the massive doors opened to reveal three almost-identical young men.

"Well, hello," Boy #1 greeted her with overfamiliar appreciation.

"What can *we* do for *you*?" Boy #2 asked suggestively.

"Name it, and it's yours," Boy #3 pledged with juvenile confidence.

Ah, the infamous Sharp triplets…living up to every wild-oat-sewing, youthfully ignorant, only-the-good-die-young description she'd heard of them since her move to Green Hills. They were precisely as she'd expected: rich and spoiled.

Blake fought the urge to wipe the smug grins off their tanned, chiseled faces.

*Stay professional; everything rides on this sale.*

"I'm looking for Mr. Sharp, please," she requested, holding her chin high and her shoulders back. Their wealth and entitlement did not intimidate her.

"It's your lucky day," Boy #1 said.

"You found him," Boy #2 leered.

"Mr. *Hudson* Sharp?"

"Aw, man. Why do the hot ones always want to talk to Hud?" Boy #3 grumbled.

"We'll go get him," the three boys offered simultaneously, their unified voices revealing their disappointment.

"Thank you," she called to the backs of the trio as they walked away, leaving her to peruse the foyer.

Blake ran a hand over more intricate carvings on the wall paneling beside the front doors. After absorbing the sun through the oversized windows on either side of the entry-way, the smooth wood warmed her chilled skin. She admired an oil painting of a cowboy and a woman beside a stream, which hung over a set of metal hooks holding rain-coats and cowboy hats. Someone had placed a large crystal vase of lush and vibrant winter flowers in the center of a round mahogany table, which was impressive in both size and quality. Had her friend Jinx Malone made the gorgeous table? Or perhaps his grandad had, when Duke could still do woodwork. Blake pressed her weight onto both hands, palms flat on the entryway table, as she leaned forward to reach the bouquet and test the flowers' perfume. Eyes closed, Blake inhaled the fresh floral fragrance. She'd just lifted onto her tiptoes to get a little closer to the heavenly scent when the authoritative clip of boot heels against the stained concrete floor alerted Blake to someone coming her way.

———

Those blasted boys would've abandoned the stranger in the foyer all night if Hudson had left it to them to get rid of her. Therefore, he had no choice but to confront the lady. Letting his steps thunder down the hall to signal he didn't appreciate the disruption, Hudson opened his mouth to roar whatever it took to make her go away when the sprite of a woman stopped him in his tracks.

Light filtering through the front doors' sidelight windows cast a glow around her, head to high-heeled toe. Bouncy waves of layered auburn hair draped to cover her face as she leaned over to smell the flowers Anita, the housekeeper's daughter, liked to put all around the house when she came to cook for them a few times each week.

Balanced on her hands, she rested her hips against the edge of the wooden table like a gymnast on the uneven bars. Both her feet dangled above the floor, one leg bent, one leg straight. After inhaling a breath so deep her shoulders lifted, she slowly lowered her feet back to the earth and shifted her weight from her arms.

With one hand, the woman ran her fingers along the tendrils hanging at her temple to hold them out of her way. As she continued the gesture, tucking her hair behind her ear, a wave of awareness and a tingle of *something* ran down Hudson's spine. When she closed her eyes for a brief pause, maybe to inhale the bouquet's fragrance one last time, or possibly shoring up patience and strength, his pulse quickened. His breath caught.

Then his enchantress looked his way, and Hudson Sharp's heart stopped completely.

**2**

*The stiletto is a feminine weapon
that men just don't have.*
**Christian Louboutin**

"Mr. Sharp?" Blake asked, straightening and stepping around the exquisite table to extend her hand toward the rather tall, totally overbearing, ridiculously pompous man in front of her. Had to be him: Hudson Alexander Sharp IV.

"Yes, I am," he answered, shaking her hand. A frisson of excitement crept up her arm. She attributed it to nerves. "May I help you?" he asked.

"I'm Blake Fish—"

"In that case," the man interrupted, his head cocked in obvious disappointment and his voice tinged with resignation, "get out. And don't come back." He turned to walk away without even allowing her to finish saying her name.

"Mr. Sharp," Blake started, halting his progress with a hand to his arm. "I've been trying to reach you. Please, may we speak for a moment?"

"No."

"I have a business proposal to share with you."

"I don't care," he said, removing her fingers from around his bicep and turning again to leave.

"It's a lucrative offer. Please hear me out," Blake called as he walked away. She drew the line at begging, but stressed urgency strained her voice, all the same. "My clients are purchasing a plot of land beside the southeast border of your property. They'd like to make you an offer for a small section of the acreage adjacent to it, the area planted with Christmas trees."

"Not interested," he called over one shoulder.

Blake's mere presence must've offended him greatly, as he couldn't be bothered to hesitate or even look her in the eye as he dismissed her.

"You haven't heard the offer," she said, hastening to catch him in the hallway. She'd worked too hard to get to this point to let it all fall apart because of one bull-headed, rich, snobby jerk.

Pivoting on one heel, Hudson Sharp turned cool, direct eyes on her.

"No, I haven't," he agreed, but his tone sent shivers up her arms. "And I don't need to hear it. I'm *not interested*. You may see yourself out, since you obviously know the way." With that, he clipped his heels right back down the hall and disappeared into a room at the end.

The heavy click of Hudson Sharp closing the door echoed through Blake like the final clang of a nail being hammered into her coffin.

*M*r. High & Mighty didn't need to hear her offer, but Blake desperately needed to present it.

During the fall of 2019, the Davenport sisters and their friend Mary Beth Carmichael had approached Blake to purchase the Wimberly Glass Factory, a dilapidated warehouse and the twenty acres of commercial-zoned land that went with it. The afternoon the ladies had reached out for Blake's help on the transaction had been mere hours after she'd accepted that moving to Green Hills had been a mistake, that her dream of owning and operating a real estate brokerage had died, and that she had failed. Miserably.

In a flash, they'd changed her situation, her stars, and her life. That phone call from Janie Lyn Davenport had not only breathed life into Blake's financial projections, it had buoyed Blake's hopes for her future.

Then, last Christmas, Janie Lyn had called again, asking her to write an enormous contract to purchase a portion of the established tree farm next to the glass factory. Since then, complications had delayed the deal time and again, due to COVID-19.

And almost a year later, Blake's success as a business owner and her ability to stay in Green Hills depended upon closing the Davenport/Carmichael deal. Soon.

Unfortunately, closing that deal depended upon Blake convincing the Sharp family to part with a tiny sliver of their precious Twin Oaks. Blake's clients had decided they didn't want one property without the other.

Therefore, Blake couldn't afford to give up.

She squared her shoulders and marched right down the vast hallway, ignoring both the resplendent artwork on the walls and the erratic beating of her heart. Hudson Sharp *would* listen to her — she wouldn't take *no* for an answer.

Not stopping to knock on the closed door for fear she'd

chicken out, Blake gripped the weighty bronze handle, turned it, and charged into the most impressive library she'd ever seen.

Her eyes scanned two stories of floor-to-ceiling book-shelves, each level at least sixteen feet tall. Multiple ladders on rollers and weathered metal rails connected to the shelves. Blake would've loved losing herself amidst the magnificent collection of books, but the moment her gaze collided with Hudson's, she refocused her determination and steeled her spine for battle.

"Ms. Fisher," he began, all Lord-of-the-Manor-ish, "I believe I left no doubt as to my wishes when I asked you to leave. Immediately. And to never step foot on Twin Oaks again."

"Why?"

"I thought that was obvious: I don't want you here." He stood from the oversized leather chair in which he'd been sitting, behind an enormous desk, again mahogany and again stunning. Hudson looked almost identical to his brothers: tall with broad shoulders, tanned skin from a life lived outdoors, sandy brown hair worn naturally mussed on top but clipped shorter in the back and on the sides. He emanated a rugged energy barely harnessed by his barreled chest, solid build, and chiseled jaw. On Hudson, the lean and wiry strength his younger brothers carried had matured into stability — capability. To say Hudson filled out his jeans and button-down pearl-snap shirt would've been an undeniable understatement. He wore authority like an invisible duster, which only added to his virile physique.

He also filled the space, making the extensive library feel intimate, and making Blake feel much smaller than her five-foot-six frame — five-foot-ten counting her stilettos. Just as when she'd stood under the twin oaks guarding the ranch entrance, Blake held no allusions as to who was in charge.

"Yes," she acknowledged with a shaky gulp, "you've made

that abundantly clear." Refusing to cower, Blake walked to his desk, mirrored his defiant stance, and looked directly into his deep, evergreen eyes. "I'm more curious as to why you won't even speak with me? Or hear why I've worked so hard to talk to you?"

"Like I said, there's no need."

That was his entire explanation, which made a rebuttal challenging. Luckily, Blake excelled at arguing.

"I'm sure that's how you see it—"

"That's how it is," he interrupted with finality.

"—Mr. Sharp," Blake continued, speaking over him to trudge forward. "But my clients have constructed a sound business plan to reconstruct the burnt warehouse that used to be Wimberly Glass, that is currently a hazard and an eyesore. The retail experience they have laid out will benefit all parties involved, *including* the entire Green Hills community *and* Twin Oaks. Their vision is built upon the beauty of the surrounding tree farm; they can't make one work without the other. They—"

He cut her off again. "I'm fully aware of their vision to create a Christmas shopping Mecca, right here in Green Hills." The mounting pressure of the steam in her head threatened to blow any minute, just like the cartoon characters who lost their cool in the Sunday comics.

"Then you're also fully aware my clients have the financial backing and resources to make this a very successful business venture."

"I have no doubt it'll be a big hit… Max wouldn't let his wife jump off this cliff if he didn't think it was a winnable game plan."

Wouldn't *let* his wife? Jump off a cliff? If *a man* didn't think it was a *winnable game plan*?

"Mr. Hudson," Blake began, trying valiantly to rein in her

indignation, her frustration, her temper, and her urge to scream. "You should kno—"

"In fact, I'm sure it will be fabulous, a real coup for the Davenports and a great tourist trap to bring in holiday shoppers. It's just not going to happen anywhere near Twin Oaks."

He'd done it *again*. Blake couldn't get a word in edgewise! Not that the buffoon possessed any reasoning skills or ability to listen, even if she got through a full sentence without him rudely and obnoxiously cutting her off.

"Instead of zero soil management and a burnt-out metal building creating an ugly backdrop from the highway, wouldn't you rather have beautiful log buildings, an award-winning restaurant, and conscientious oversight of the land next to Twin Oaks? Their plan—"

"How do you know the buildings will be beautiful?"

Blake fought ridiculously powerful impulses to stomp her foot. And strangle the man.

"What makes you think the designs will be aesthetically in line with the rustic terrain?" he continued. "Who said Mary Beth Carmichael's next restaurant will win awards? And exactly who, Ms. Fisher, do you think approves soil management plans in Pittsburg County?"

While listing his questions — nay, *accusations* — Hudson Sharp walked around the stately desk. Each slow, deliberate step brought him closer and closer, until only a fraction of air separated the adversaries.

*Please, Lord, glue my feet to this spot on the ground and do not let him see me sweat*, Blake prayed.

"I know those things by faith, Mr. Sharp," she answered with unyielding confidence. "I believe in my clients; I trust in their vision. I"—Blake drew out the emphasis on herself with a hand splayed over her heart —"might be newer to Green Hills than the illustrious Sharp family, but I have come to know, love, and depend upon this place. I'd imagine I appreciate the community here much as your ancestors did when they settled the area and established the town six generations ago: hardworking, kind, supportive, and dependable. In fact, *Doctor Sharp*" —Blake paused just long enough to cast a disdainful glance at his gallery of diplomas on the wall, the largest and most ornately framed document announcing to the world he'd earned a PhD in Crop, Soil, and Management Sciences from Auburn University— "I'd even go so far as to suggest you're not the only human on earth capable of determining what's good for the soil, the fields, the farmers, the ranchers, and the townsfolk of Green Hills."

Since she didn't have a mic to drop, Blake made do with a haughty hair flip and the snappy staccato of her red patent leather high heels on the hardwood floor as she left Doctor Hudson Alexander Sharp — *the Fourth* — speechless.

## 3

*Enemies are so stimulating.*
**Katharine Hepburn**

She'd done her research. Hudson gave her that.

After tormenting him with endless voicemails, emails, letters through the post office, and even DMs on the ranch's social media accounts, the insufferable Blake Fisher — real estate agent extraordinaire — had snuck her way onto Twin Oaks, finagled an invitation inside the Big House, and given Hudson the "what for."

She wasn't afraid to speak her mind. Hudson could give her that, too.

Hudson *wasn't* willing to concede that she'd left with the upper hand. Or that his heart had skipped a few beats on multiple occasions during Ms. Fisher's visit. And he absolutely wasn't willing to admit he'd been wrong in ignoring the spirited and stunning woman for the past several months.

When her first dozen or so letters and emails had arrived in January, Hudson had assumed Blake Fisher was a man. When the world came to an abrupt halt in March and the queries ceased, Hudson had forgotten all about the real estate agent. And when the letters started back up in September, he'd trashed each one without a second's hesitation.

Ignoring the problem hadn't fixed the problem. Somehow, she'd uncovered his cell phone number and begun leaving voicemails. It was then he'd heard her voice and realized his mistake regarding the agent's gender.

Standing under a golden ray of sunshine in the entryway of the Big House at Twin Oaks, she'd moved the veil of her thick, wavy golden-red hair to reveal honey-toned skin that rivaled porcelain and hazel eyes that sparkled with brilliant flecks matching the highlights in her hair. Right then, Hudson had realized the immense magnitude of his mistake.

Blake Fisher was *not* a man.

*L*eaning back in the supple leather chair with his boots propped on his desk, Hudson studied the library ceiling. He was enjoying his solitude — maybe sparing a thought or two for his unexpected visitor — when his brothers burst in without an invitation. That seemed to be going around.

"Who's the hottie?"

"Really, Tobias? It's 2020," Hudson reprimanded triplet #1, lifting his feet from their place of rest and planting them on the floor. He sat tall in his chair to face the boys. "I'm pretty sure you'd be strung up by your toes if anyone heard you say that in public."

"Babe?"

"Not any better, Karl," Hudson quipped, shaking his head and flashing a look of disdain at triplet #2.

"How about fox?"

"You're getting really good at tying your own noose, Bennie," Hudson retorted, raising a judgmental eyebrow at triplet #3. Hudson shuffled papers on his desk to appear busy. The boys didn't take the hint.

"Then what are we supposed to call her?" Tobi questioned.

"She *is* a super hot…" Karl added.

"Foxy babe!" Bennie said, completing their complaint.

When the boys spoke as one unit, Hudson worried they also shared one brain. Perhaps only one brain cell, at that.

"I'm no expert, but I believe women want to be respected for their intellect, accomplishments, and personality — rather than being nicknamed for their physical attributes. That particular woman is Ms. Blake Fisher. She's the real estate agent blowing us up about selling land to developers, and you three are to avoid her at all costs," Hudson warned, with a direct, hear-my-words glare at each of his brothers in turn.

"But—" all three of them voiced in sync.

"Period," Hudson barked. "Now, go — anywhere but here. I have work to do, and y'all are nothing if not distracting."

"Hudson?" Tobi asked from the doorway.

"Yeah?" he answered without looking up from the file he pretended to read.

"If ladies don't want to be known for their physical attributes…" Karl prefaced.

"Then why do they look so pretty and smell so nice?" Bennie finished for the trio.

Luckily, the boys meandered off without waiting for an answer.

*W*ith the coast clear, Hudson rocked back in his chair, stacked his boot heels on the desk, and clasped his hands behind his head. He resumed his contemplation of the ceiling — and of Ms. Blake Fisher.

The boys had a valid point: the saucy little spitfire *was* gorgeous.

And courageous.

More than one grown man had retreated when confronted with Hudson's infamous grumpiness and snarling demeanor. Not Blake Fisher. She hadn't backed down, hadn't even winced when going toe to toe with him.

But she hadn't been unfazed, either.

Hudson hadn't missed the moment she lifted her pert, button nose a little higher into the air. She had a tendency to worry her full bottom lip — a nervous gesture that revealed a faint scar above her mouth, one which made her top lip infinitesimally lopsided. Hudson expected he'd be seeing the delicate beauty mark placed just below the corner of her lips in his dreams...as well as the rat-a-tat rhythm of her heartbeat pulsating along the silky skin of her delicate neck.

Unfortunately, though —and contrary to the boys' clueless commentary — Blake Fisher was more than just a pretty face. Much more.

The navy pinstripe suit she wore expressed consummate professionalism. A strand of pearls and matching stud earrings illustrated classiness. Her ivory silk blouse, loosely tied at the neck to look prim and proper, hinted at a romantic nature. Those ankle-breaking four-inch scarlet stilettos told their own story.

*Keep your friends close, but your enemies closer.*

Hudson had read the proverb in Sun Tzu's *The Art of War*, and he'd heard it again from Michael Corleone in *Godfather II*. He considered both to be authoritative resources.

She'd obviously done her homework. Hudson needed to do the same.

He opened his laptop, clicked on a web browser, and had barely typed her name in the search bar when Bennie popped his head into the library.

"She's still here," he told Hudson.

"Benjamin, for the bazillionth time, knock first," Hudson growled. "And what do you mean, *she's still here*? Surely, back-tracking one's path to the frontage road that leads to town isn't too much to ask!"

"Ms. Fisher" —Benjamin looked quite proud that he'd called her by an appropriate name— "might've started down that path, but she only made it as far as the arena. Tobi and Karl are practicing, and she's right there at the fence, watching 'em team rope."

"In her power suit, pearls, and red high heels?"

"Yep, that's her."

"Serves her right to be covered in dust," Hudson blustered under his breath. "I've got a little more work to do here," he said, speaking to Bennie, but looking back at the image of Blake Fisher on his screen. "See if you have any more luck running her off than I did. If you don't, I'll be there in a bit to do it myself. Again."

"Will do," Bennie agreed. But Hudson didn't acknowledge him, or even hear the door close when his brother left. An old article in *The Gazette* announcing a new real estate company in town monopolized Hudson's attention.

**Green Hills Welcomes Front Porch Realty**
**February 28, 2019**

**Residents of Green Hills, Pittsburg County, and the**

*surrounding areas are elated to welcome Front Porch Realty to the community. Located at 308 South Pin Oak Lane, the new real estate company is officially open for business. Be sure to stop by soon to meet owner, operator, and lead real estate agent Blake Fisher, who specializes in residential listings, buyers' agency, and property management.*

*Born and raised in Alabama, Fisher moved to Oklahoma City last August, when she accepted a job managing a branch office for OklaFirst Real Estate & Property Management. Working in that role, Fisher discovered a passion for leading a team and a desire to build her own business outside the big city. Fond memories of visiting Daisy Lake one summer as a child brought the real estate agent and sales broker back to Green Hills. "There's something special here, a uniqueness of character and charisma I've never witnessed in any other community. The moment I stepped out of my car and explored Green Hills, I knew I'd found my home," Fisher told The Gazette.*

*Green Hills Mayor Stacia Howell is thrilled to see another independently owned and operated boutique business choose Green Hills for their home base. "What a wonderful addition to our town! With Front Porch Realty right off Main Street and Blake's knowledge and experience, residents and rental property owners no longer need to look elsewhere for help with their real estate transactions. It's a win-win for all," says Howell.*

*The mayor and representatives from the Green Hills Chamber of Commerce will be on hand for an official ribbon-cutting ceremony to kick off a grand opening celebration slated for tomorrow, Friday, March 1, from 4–6 p.m. All are invited to stop by the come-and-go event.*

How had Hudson missed all the hoopla back then? Blake Fisher had arrived in Green Hills twenty-two months ago, and in all that time, he'd never laid eyes upon her.

*I need to get out more.*

Even before his parents' midlife change of plans, Hudson had rarely ventured too far from Twin Oaks. The ranch checked all his boxes: a home and office in which to live and work, land to toil upon, animals to raise, ponds and streams full of fish to catch, plenty of wildlife to hunt, fruit trees and vegetable gardens to harvest, air to breathe, and space to think. What else could a person want?

His mother often argued Hudson needed a companion. She swore up and down he lived an incomplete life, simply because he had yet to — as she liked to put it — *find true love.* Hudson saw right through the argument… Already bored with retirement, she'd decided a new generation of Sharps to spoil would bring her great joy… She wanted Hudson to supply her with grandbabies, and sooner rather than later.

A vision of a toddler floated through his mind. A little boy walking by his side — wanting to "work" and refusing to be left behind — in tiny blue jeans and miniature boots, with a straw hat on his head and a shortened rope in his pudgy hand. Then an image popped into his head of a sweet and feisty little girl, wearing a ruffled sundress and boots with thick braids under her hat. She gripped Hudson's little finger while they walked to the barn to feed the horses as the sun rose on an early morning. He couldn't help but enjoy the images.

Flashes of the future?

Or unattainable dreams?

Either way, he didn't have time for wool-gathering... Hudson had a thistle festering that would only get more painful if he didn't get rid of it, one in the form of an undeniably super hot, foxy babe who — according to all he'd seen and read online — was too smart, too savvy, and too determined for her own good.

Or at least for Hudson's.

## 4

> *There is no secret so close*
> *as that between a rider and his horse.*
> **Robert Smith Surtees**

Fascinated by two boys riding their horses like hounds on the trail of their prey's scent, Blake slowed her car to watch as she drove past the arena. When she witnessed them roping a sweet, innocent calf in full stride of a gallop, she stopped the car to look closer.

On one hand, they — the horses and riders alike — amazed her. The fluidity with which they rode stunned Blake. Each rider and horse moved flawlessly across the hard-packed earth as a single being. They seemed to possess a sixth sense, knowing their role by instinct such that their balance never wavered. On the other hand, she worried about that little cow.

"Well, hello, pretty lady," a voice catcalled from behind Blake.

She glanced over her shoulder with a glower of disgust firmly in place.

Great…triplet #3.

Without a response, she turned her attention back to the arena.

"Hudson sent me to give you the boot," the boy said, sidling up to the fence next to her. He reached down to tug a tall weed from the grass at their feet, stuck the end in his mouth, propped his forearms on the top rail of the fence, and rested one booted foot on the bottom rail. "But I can't blame you for stopping to watch — they're magic in motion, aren't they?"

A thread of respect lifted the young man's voice. He didn't sound nearly so awful once he dropped the sugary charm he used in his attempt to appear cool and worldly.

"Are they hurting that baby cow?" Blake asked.

"No," he answered. "Tobi and Karl are practicing exactly how we rope cattle in the field. And the calf wears that helmet to protect his neck. We don't wrestle and tie 'em unless we have to out in the pasture."

"But they're practicing an event for a rodeo, aren't they? Isn't that just for sport?"

"Yes. And no," he answered again. "They are practicing their event, and it's true they compete in rodeos to see who does it best, but it's not just for sport. Cowboys have been going up against the clock and Mother Nature for hundreds of years. Doing it for official time and in front of a crowd showcases skills that keep a ranch running, keeps beef in the grocery stores, and keeps dinner on the table. Besides all that, us being good at our events is paying for our college through rodeo scholarships."

"I'm pretty sure y'all could've found a way to pay for books and tuition," Blake said, raising one eyebrow as she looked at him with a smirk.

The boy chuckled in agreement. "That's true," he allowed. "But we've worked hard to earn those scholarships, and we're all three really proud to be on one of the top rodeo teams in all of college athletics."

"Which is which?" she asked.

"What d'ya mean?"

"You said Karl and Tobi. Which is which?"

"Ah, Tobi — Tobias — is the oldest of us; he's the header, so he ropes the calf's horns or around his neck. Karl is the middle triplet; he's the heeler, so he follows Karl and ropes the back end of the calf. Anywhere behind the shoulders is legal."

"Tobi's in the blue-striped shirt, and Karl is in the brown plaid?"

"You got it," he confirmed.

"And who are you?" Blake faced the youngest Sharp, taking the time to really look at him, to see him as a person instead of an irritating, spoiled rich kid.

"Benjamin Tyrell Sharp," he announced with a big grin, "at your service." He extended his hand, so she shook it. When she tried to release his hand, he tightened his grip, prompting her to look askance at the boy.

"But my friends call me Bennie," he told her with a wink. The oozy charm had returned.

"Well, *Benjamin*," she said, retrieving her hand from his grasp, "it's nice to meet you." She allowed a genuine smile to accompany her slight barb of using his full name. "Do you rope, too?"

"Everyone on a working ranch rides and ropes, but I don't enter roping events anymore. I compete in bareback riding… Where it's just me and the horse. He gives me his worst, and I try to ride my best. In the end, we see who wins. On a good day, we both do."

The reverence in Benjamin's voice left no question as to his love for his sport. The more genuine side of the young man intrigued Blake, even if he came from the highfalutin Sharp dynasty. Obviously, they were all repulsively privileged and spoiled rotten. But perhaps Benjamin had been saved from airs of self-entitlement. Honestly, he seemed pretty down to earth.

"Do you ride?" he asked, shaking Blake from her musings.

"Me? Oh, no," she stuttered. "Horses are exquisite, but they're not for me."

"If you're gonna be 'round here for more than a minute, you gotta ride. I can teach you," he offered.

"To ride a horse? Like they are?" Incredulity spiked her voice an octave higher than usual.

"Yep— Well, maybe not like *they* are. But in a way you'll feel safe and secure in the saddle. I have the perfect horse for you: Ethel. She's slow and sweet and gentle and kind. Her temperament's opposite the alpha mare — which would be Lucy. You'll love—"

"Wait," Blake interrupted, lifting a hand to stop his description. "You named your horses Lucy and Ethel?"

"Mom did. She's a huge fan of *I Love Lucy*." Benjamin did that amused chuckle of his again. "We've all seen every episode, but Mom's seen them a million times and can recite every line. Watching her watch the show is funnier than the actual television program. She knows everything they're going to say before they say it, yet she laughs so hard she's crying at them every single time. It's hysterical."

Blake couldn't deny Benjamin adored his mother. Maybe the Sharps were more normal a family than she'd allowed. If the infamous Sharp triplets indulged their mother in watching and rewatching vintage sitcom reruns, they couldn't be too bratty.

"Where is your mom? And your dad? When I tried getting in touch with the owner of that land by the old Wimberly Glass property, I heard your parents were on an extended trip." Blake hoped he mistook her prying nosiness for interest rather than a fishing expedition.

"They're living it up on the high seas," he answered easily, and with another fond smile. "When they called on Thanksgiving, they'd turned the yacht toward the Virgin Islands, so they must be floating somewhere in the Atlantic. That's supposed to be great sailing in December."

BAM — there it was: highbrow aristocracy at its worst. *That* fit Blake's perception of the illustrious Sharps of Twin Oaks.

"Handing out family secrets, Bennie?" The deep yet grumpy voice behind Blake and Benjamin could only belong to one person.

"Oh, hey, Hudson," Benjamin answered, completely unfazed by his older brother's censure. "Ms. Fisher was just asking about Mom and Dad."

"I bet she was," Hudson commented, insinuating the worst — even if he wasn't wrong in the accusation. Her attempt to gather intel might've been lost on one Sharp brother, but not the other.

"Actually, Ms. Fisher and I were just making plans," Benjamin declared, which prompted both Blake and Hudson to look at the boy in confusion.

"We were?" she asked.

"You were?" Hudson also asked, at the same moment. That prompted the two adversaries to glower at one another.

"Yep," Benjamin continued, oblivious to the tension zapping between Blake and Hudson. Ah, to be young and ignorant. "I'm going to teach her to ride."

## 5

**Better than a thousand days of diligent study**
**is one day with a great teacher.**
***Japanese proverb***

"In *that*?" Hudson looked Ms. Fisher up and down, not hiding his mixed emotions of both appreciation and contempt.

"Nah," the boy answered for her. "We'll start another day. How 'bout tomorrow?" Bennie asked, turning his attention from Hudson to Ms. Fisher. "You have some boots and jeans?"

"Of course. I have a pair of cowboy boots. And jeans that go with them," Blake answered, speaking to Bennie, although her eyes remained locked with Hudson's.

He tilted his chin just enough to challenge her. He didn't hide his annoyance that Bennie had gone and done *exactly* what Hudson had instructed the boys *not* to do: go anywhere near Ms. Blake Fisher. She had to know Hudson wanted — *expected* — her to decline Bennie's offer. Did she have it in her to go against his blatant wishes?

"Tomorrow sounds lovely," the audacious little witch had the nerve to say. Her sugary sweet smile — aimed directly at Hudson rather than at Bennie, to whom she spoke — revealed all Hudson needed to know: she'd agreed to Bennie's hare-brained scheme just to get under Hudson's skin. "What time should I arrive?"

"I'll finish feeding and chores around 8 a.m. — is that too early?" Pure joy and excitement lit up Bennie's eyes. He might be harebrained, but he loved to introduce newbies to horses, to share his wonder in their beauty. Hard to fault the kid for that.

"Sounds perfect," Ms. Fisher replied, finally bestowing an authentic smile upon Bennie. "I hope I won't disappoint you. I'm not as sure as you seem to be that I can master horseback riding." Her heart pounded. Hudson saw the rhythm in her neck. He didn't want her around Twin Oaks, but he also didn't want her to be nervous or scared, especially to ride.

"No better instructor than Bennie," Hudson informed her. "You're in excellent hands."

"Well then," she agreed, "I guess I'll be back tomorrow."

With a slight nod, she walked away from the men.

She'd only gone a few steps when Hudson added, "Legally."

"Excuse me?" Ms. Fisher turned to ask, one brow lifted with a snootiness that had come to naturally.

"Can you remember 018810? It's the gate code. You'll need it to get onto Twin Oaks — *legally* this time."

She didn't deign to respond to his reference to her trespassing. Instead, she frowned upon him before pivoting on one red high heel with an expressive hair toss — as she had in his office earlier — and marched to her vehicle.

Blake Fisher didn't spare him another glance, but Hudson watched — contemplating — as she drove away.

*Friday, December 11, 2020*

rom his perch on Justice, Hudson enjoyed an unobstructed view of Ms. Fisher arriving for her riding lesson. After checking on water levels for the cattle at dawn, he'd given his majestic four-year-old dark chestnut stallion free rein to go wherever he chose. After a refreshing gallop, they'd ended up at the top of a high rolling hill, where sturdy oaks camouflaged Hudson from others, but where he could see the barns, the paddock, and the practice arena. The December air had a bite to it, but without a breeze, the sun's budding rays made the spot quite perfect for spectating.

After winding her way from the ranch entrance to the stables, Ms. Fisher parked next to the open doors at the barn. She stepped from her car, and Hudson surveyed her attire from top to bottom. She wore a navy-and-green-plaid wool vest over a heavy ivory turtleneck sweater. Her blue jeans — snug in all the right places — widened at the hem to cover distressed cowboy boots. Hudson couldn't be certain from that distance, but it appeared they had colorful flowers embroidered on the leather. Fancy, girly, go-dancing-at-Scooter's boots. *Not* riding boots.

At least she was smart enough to dress according to the weather, Hudson conceded, when Ms. Fisher tugged a thick ivory beanie — one with a goofy fake-fur pom-pom on top — over her mass of auburn hair, the waves easily reaching the middle of her back. Rays of sunlight reflected off the beanie and illuminated golden highlights in the strands of her hair. In effect, she glowed and her silky tresses sparkled. She lit up the world around her.

Hudson grumbled.

Focusing on *not* noticing her, just as he'd concentrated on *not* thinking about her since coming face-to-face with her,

Hudson turned Justice away from the barn and the offensive people in it and nudged his horse toward Aunt Juni's trees. The acreage wasn't far from the barn — another argument for *not* selling any of his family's land to anyone, much less someone inviting droves of strangers to the land. At an easy canter, Hudson and Justice reached the outer edge of the Christmas trees within ten minutes.

*Not, not, not…* The word bounced around his head. Hudson had thought and said it more in the past eighteen hours than he had in as many months. That blasted woman pushed Hudson to be the most negative of people.

He grumbled again.

Why did the Davenport ladies need *his* land? There were other parcels of land for sale around Green Hills and throughout Pittsburg County, land that didn't back up to Twin Oaks. Why couldn't they set up their Christmas business some-where else? Somewhere *not* near Twin Oaks.

Probably because his land was the best.

Ambling Justice further into Juni's woods, Hudson inhaled a deep breath. The winter air, scented with evergreens and rich earth, filled his lungs and balanced his senses. Light filtered through the treetops, creating a glistening aura of mystique, quite similar to the way sunlight had illuminated the woman who wanted to ruin this perfect peace by welcoming people into his haven. In no time at all they'd be trampling the pine needles, scaring away the animals, and filling the space with the cacophony of chattering adults, boisterous children, and squealing babies. Imagining the scene turned Hudson's stomach.

Whatever it took, he had to protect Twin Oaks.

Hackles raised, Hudson nudged Justice toward the barn and urged him to go faster until they galloped full speed to ensure they made it there before time cooled his irritation. He practiced what he'd say to her, explaining in no uncertain terms that every inch of Twin Oaks land would remain with the ranch. He'd make her understand there would be no negotiating, no terms, no contract, and absolutely no sale. Ms. Fisher could click her sexy stilettos, sashay in her figure-hugging blue jeans, and shake her luscious auburn locks all she wanted. He didn't care. Hudson wasn't interested. In fact, he was completely immune to—

Her charms.

Hudson topped the final ridge before the paddock and brought Justice to an immediate halt.

Spine straight, hips relaxed, heels down, Ms. Fisher sat perfectly in the saddle. A huge smile of unadulterated pleasure brightened her expression. Bennie said something Hudson couldn't make out from so far away, and Ms. Fisher laughed in response. The cheerful lilt of her joy floated on the air. *That* Hudson heard as clear as a bell.

Lured like a sailor to a siren's song, he nudged Justice into motion and trotted down the rise to join teacher and pupil in the paddock.

"I see you're a schemer *and* a liar," Hudson said in place of a greeting.

"Hud—" Bennie questioned, obviously taken aback by such a blatant display of rudeness.

"Excuse me?" Ms. Fisher demanded over Bennie's protest, her tone even more outraged than when she'd said the same thing the day before.

"First, you trespass on the ranch. Then you claim you don't know how to ride a horse, finagling lessons from Bennie to get yourself back onto the ranch," Hudson accused. "He's a good teacher, but no one is that good. You've obviously ridden before."

"Hud—" Bennie began again.

"So you're angry that I'm here? Or that I'm staying in the

saddle? Which is it, Mr. Lord and Master?" Ms. Fisher demanded over Bennie's second attempt to rein in Hudson.

"Both," Hudson answered succinctly.

"Blake's a quick study, Hud. Really — she's done great. We were just headed out to a trail, so she doesn't have to keep going in circles," Bennie said, speaking as quickly as Hudson had ever heard his most laid-back brother talk.

"Wonderful," Hudson spewed. "I'll come with you."

"Great! We can—" Bennie tried to comment as he swung onto Topper's saddle.

"Must you?" Ms. Fisher questioned over him. Dislike dripped from each word.

Hudson didn't bother to answer, instead pointing Justice toward an established riding trail in the woods just beyond the practice arena, effectively taking the lead.

"Bennie, ride ahead and open the gates to the eastern park."

"*Please?*" Ms. Fisher reprimanded under her breath — yet loud enough for all to hear — scolding Hudson's manners, or lack thereof.

After Bennie cantered off, Hudson slowed until Justice walked beside Ethel.

"Why'd you lie? The boys might drive me crazy, but they're good kids. Bennie's by far the most gullible of the three — determined to believe the best in everyone. He doesn't deserve your manipulation; he won't see it for what it is, and frankly, he'll be blindsided when you show your true colors."

"Wow," Ms. Fisher scoffed. "You clearly don't share Bennie's faith in the world. How does a rich kid who's been given everything on a silver spoon his entire life grow into such an arrogant, cynical, nasty grown-up? You are without a doubt the most insufferable, vitriolic human I've ever had the misfortune to know."

"You *don't* know me," Hudson pointed out.

"And yet you *think* you know me," she countered.

"Where'd you learn to ride?"

"In that arena next to your barn. About an hour ago."

Hudson studied her face, ferreting out the truth. Even with her lips pursed tight in antipathy, he couldn't deny the woman's exquisite beauty. It didn't make Hudson feel any better about her. A girl who looked like that would know exactly how to use those looks to her advantage. Take poor Bennie for instance... He'd fallen at her feet in no time flat.

Hudson continued to stare.

Ms. Fisher's eyes met his. They held a trace of nerves and a healthy dose of disdain. But she didn't display the outward signs of someone lying. And the rest of her body remained perfectly postured, with the reins loose in her left hand, her chin high, and her hips relaxed to match Ethel's natural gait.

"Other than pony rides at the county fair and one week at a summer camp when I was maybe eleven years old, today is the only time I've ridden a horse. It's certainly the first time I've been on one long enough for someone to actually teach me *how* to ride. You should give Bennie more credit; he explained what I needed to do to make Ethel comfortable in words I related to. He was patient and unruffled in his corrections. Instead of rebuffing my nervousness, he helped me channel that energy into excitement without my scaring the horse, so neither Ethel nor I were skittish."

"I'm well aware of Bennie's talents. We host riding camps over the summer for children with disabilities and special needs. Bennie is always the most popular instructor," Hudson told Ms. Fisher. "He has a gift for putting people at ease around the horses, and he's affable and easygoing. I pray every day he'll discover a way to put those skills to good use."

"Then why all the unfounded accusations leveled at me?"

"Your body alignment is near perfect; you move in instant rhythm with Ethel's natural gait. Those aren't things anyone can learn in an hour. Not even Bennie could teach you that kind of body control," Hudson explained.

"Thank you?" Ms. Fisher questioned. "I think there was a compliment in there somewhere." She glanced at Hudson, lifting one eyebrow and leveling her own accusation his way. He half shrugged, and she looked down at the ground in front of Ethel as she continued, "I'd guess the body control comes from sports. I swam every second of every summer when I was a kid. When I got to junior high, I ran track, specifically the hurdles and pole vault. Part of my training included gymnastics. Alignment and posture awareness are critical in those activities. Now I practice yoga daily, so I'm still very in tune with my body."

"Do you like it?" Hudson asked.

"My yoga practice? I love it," she answered.

"No, riding. What do you think?" For some reason Hudson refused to consider, her answer mattered. He wanted her to enjoy being on a horse. He hoped she appreciated Ethel's easy clip-clop meandering, the scent of the pines and the earthy ranch air. Hudson needed Ms. Fisher to understand for herself why he simply didn't have it in him to part with even a sliver of Twin Oaks.

"I'll probably be a little sore, but the motion in the saddle isn't as jarring or uncomfortable as I thought it would be," she allowed. "And Ethel is a dear — so sweet to let me ride when surely she'd rather be nibbling oats in the warm barn."

Ms. Fisher leaned forward to rub Ethel's neck with affection that matched the respect and admiration in her voice. The length of auburn waves flowing loose below her knit beanie fell to veil her face, much as when he'd discovered her smelling the fresh flowers in the entryway of the Big House the day before. And just as it had then, when Ms. Fisher smoothed her hair away from her face, Hudson's heart skipped a beat. Smile lines crinkled at the corners of her eyes, the irises golden in the bright sunlight. Cheeks, rosy from the chilly air, accentuated soft, smooth skin. A light smattering of faint freckles highlighted her peaches-and-cream coloring. She took his breath away.

If only she wasn't also angling to take away what mattered most in his world.

## 6

*Not everything happens*
*when you expect it;*
*it is what it is.*
*The people who ride with you,*
*ride with you.*
*Kali Uchis*

Fighting the urge to give the horse a big hug as they ambled along the wooded trail, Blake patted Ethel's sinewy coat to convey her pleasure and appreciation. Ethel nickered, expressing her mutual fondness, which filled Blake with pride and joy.

"Well, at least *someone* likes me," she said, extra primly for Hudson's benefit.

He *hmm*ed a grunt, but even his sour demeanor didn't deflate Blake's good mood.

Being outdoors on such a gorgeous morning invigorated her senses. Tempted to laugh out loud and throw caution to the wind, Blake turned to Hudson with a challenge in mind.

"Can we go faster?" she asked, not wanting to tax Ethel if slow and steady was better for her.

"Well, we can't go any slower, that's for sure," he smirked.

"Is it asking too much of Ethel?"

"No," he chuckled. "She's not ready to be put out to pasture quite yet. In fact, old Ethel might just surprise you."

"Will she take off on me?" Blake's heart raced with anticipation composed of both excitement and nerves.

"Not if you don't let her."

His answer didn't inspire confidence. It wasn't even a real answer.

"Bennie did *not* get his teaching skills from you, I see."

"That was never in question." Not discounting its overriding grumpiness, Hudson's voice revealed a teeny-tiny, almost notable, even imaginable hint of amiability. "I'll control Justice. As long as you don't dig your heels into her ribs, Ethel won't do too much too fast," Hudson promised. "Move your hands up just an inch on the reins." Blake did as he said. "Now sit a little taller in the saddle and, with a nudge of your hips and heels, give her a gentle *giddyap* to trot. There you go," Hudson praised when Ethel's pace smoothly increased. "You're doing it," he congratulated her.

The warmth of his tone wreaked havoc on Blake's senses. Like warm honey, his words oozed over her. Pride at impressing him blossomed in her chest. Blake couldn't help but smile gleefully as the chilly air met her face and the crisp wind whipped through her hair. She loved it!

Hudson stayed by her side, step for step. His presence gave Blake courage. She coaxed Ethel to go a fraction faster. A giggle escaped when they reached a full-out trot.

Blake flashed a glance at Hudson. He was smiling.

And he was beautiful.

Without the menacing frown, he appeared younger…carefree. The creases around his full lips looked strong instead of tired. From beneath the brim of his cowboy hat, a playful twinkle gleamed in his eyes. Where did *this* Hudson hide? And why?

At that moment, Blake didn't care.

Fully aware of the man beside her, and fully understanding she and Ethel would never in a million years beat him and Justice, she met his gaze. Mirroring his directness, Blake issued a silent challenge to race. Then she pushed her horse to go faster.

Blake laughed out loud, spurring Ethel to go as fast as she dared to ride. The man she'd have sworn had no heart at all let Blake maintain a half-head lead as they cantered under the canopy of trees.

They remained neck and neck as they barreled deeper into the woods, rounding a curve on the trail. Suddenly, their sightline revealed Bennie and his horse stopped in the middle of the path, not more than twelve yards away. Faster than Blake could process the imminent collision, Hudson reached over and grabbed Ethel's reins from Blake's hand. He brought Justice to an instant stop and wrapped an arm around Blake's waist which halted her momentum before she toppled over Ethel's head. Both Blake's hands flew to his grasp as one hangs on to the bar of a roller coaster cart for dear life.

Ethel's hooves slid on the soft undergrowth of leaves and pine needles. Expecting to tumble onto Bennie — or worse, fall all the way to the ground — Blake braced for impact.

But it never came.

Hudson released Ethel's reins at the same time he tightened his hold on Blake, lifting her from Ethel's saddle as the horse continued forward. Graceful as a ballerina, Ethel found her footing, cut to avoid Bennie, and scrambled on until she'd gone a safe distance. There she stopped, inspected the ground at her

feet, and promptly began nibbling on winter grass edging the trail.

Meanwhile, Blake's midair suspension ended with a thud as Hudson pulled her squarely onto his lap.

Blake sat stunned.

"Are you okay?" he demanded angrily.

He glared down at her.

How could she be in trouble?

"Ye— Yes. I— I'm— I'm fine," she finally uttered. She surveyed his taut features, trying to discern what she'd done wrong. It had all happened so fast; the entire chain of events — the too near of a miss — clouded into one blurry reel in her mind. "I— I..." Blake's nerves ricocheted under the surface. She couldn't string words together. Tears burned her eyes.

She blinked quickly to prevent their overflow. Hudson's jaw clenched tighter. Blake looked down at her hands still gripping his arm around her waist. "I'm so sorry," she whispered, scared to speak any louder for fear her voice would crack and the dam restraining her emotions would break.

Hudson shifted her in his lap to see her face better. Releasing the harness of his arm, he lifted her chin with one finger. When Blake could no longer stand it, she raised her gaze to his. The naked concern in Hudson's eyes proved her undoing. Her body quaked, and tears streamed down her cheeks.

"Ah, dang it," Hudson cursed. Then he did the most un-Hudson-like thing Blake could've imagined.

Hudson High & Mighty Sharp — *the Fourth* — wrapped both his powerful arms around Blake... He tucked her into the solid wall of his chest, propped his chin on top of her head, and proceeded to soothe her fears. He whispered words of reassurance and rubbed a hand up and down her spine. Blake's breathing eventually synced with Hudson's slow rhythm of calm, deep breaths.

"Guys, I'm so sorry," Bennie stammered once Blake's emotional turmoil had run its course. "I opened all the gates like you asked, and we were headed back to meet up when Topper threw a shoe. I shouldn't have stayed smack in the middle of the trail to assess the damage to his foot. That could've been a real mess. Man, I feel awful."

"How bad is it? Can Topper walk?" Hudson asked, his voice steely but not unkind.

"Yeah, but not with extra weight. The shoe snapped clean in two, and the rest has gotta come off," Bennie explained.

"Ride Ethel to take Topper home," Hudson instructed. "We'll be there in a while."

Blake looked into Hudson's face, searching for answers to questions she didn't have the gumption to ask.

Bennie didn't ask any, either. Instead, he adjusted Ethel's stirrups, stepped into the left one, and took a seat in the saddle. He hesitated, exchanging a quick nod with Hudson, tipped his hat toward Blake, and rode off.

Just like that, she'd been abandoned in the arms of her enemy.

———

*H*udson frowned as Bennie steered Ethel and Topper toward the barn. Topper's limp could be worse; though he favored the one foot, his balance was steady. Despite that, Hudson didn't look away for a good long minute.

*Yeah, I'm stalling. I know it, Lord. Just as You do.*

The precipice on which Hudson wavered had him frozen in place. Take her back, or move forward? That was the million-dollar question.

Bennie would've been fine walking, leading Topper to the barn on foot. Hudson knew that. So did Bennie, who — thankfully — had been wise enough not to say anything.

But Hudson hadn't been ready to end his outing with Ms. Fisher just yet. Bennie had probably seen right through the situation. He wouldn't keep it to himself for long. Tongues would wag by lunchtime. Hudson hoped the lady warranted the ribbing he'd receive.

Ms. Fisher had surprised him, and that didn't occur often. For the most part, people turned out exactly as Hudson imagined they'd be: neither all good nor all bad, neither completely innocent nor unequivocally guilty, but naturally leaning one way or the other, most of the time.

He'd been so sure Ms. Fisher would prove cunning, shrewd, and devious. He'd expected her to use feminine wiles — her stunning looks and her killer body — to get whatever she wanted, at any cost. She had to know she wielded that kind of power; no one could look like that and *not* be aware of it.

Hudson hadn't counted on her being authentic or charming. He hadn't expected her to be kind, or friendly, or interested enough in others to take time to truly interact with Bennie. She was fun.

They'd been having a blast riding together — her racing and him letting her win — before they'd come upon Bennie and Topper like a deer frozen in headlights.

*Thank you, Lord, for guiding us through what could've been a disaster.*

Hudson's heart had barely recovered from the frightening what-if that had played like a movie in his mind as the scene had unfolded in real life. He'd needed a moment to compose himself after the dust settled, so he'd been more than happy to hold her tight — safe in his arms — as long as she needed.

"You sure you're okay?" he asked her once Bennie and the horses disappeared around the bend.

"Yes, thank you," she said in a voice that had regained its normal strength and command. "It was my fault. I shouldn't have been racing. I don't know these woods, and we were going *so fast*," she emphasized with regret.

*So fast?*

They'd been several gears away from that. Hudson released a slight chuckle.

She studied him with curiosity.

"Are you scared to ride now?" he asked her.

"No. Should I be? That seemed like a fluke. One that could've been avoided, at that."

"Do you trust me?" he challenged.

"You just saved my life." She smiled indulgently.

"I'll take that as a yes." Hudson paused, a hint at a smile lifting his lips. "I'm going to stand in the stirrups. You swing your leg over the saddle horn and Justice's head to take the saddle. I'll ride behind it. Ready?"

Blake nodded, and they maneuvered as smoothly as one could've hoped for. Once settled, Hudson reached both hands around her to take the reins he'd tied around the horn. He held the leather straps in his left hand, resting it on the front of the saddle. Before he could rest his right hand on his leg, Blake gripped his forearm as she had before.

In natural response, he wrapped his arm around her midsection…to be sure she felt secure. Or so he tried to convince himself. When she shifted closer, when she leaned into his chest, he acknowledged the truth: having her there simply felt good. It felt right.

"Do we weigh too much for Justice?" Blake asked.

"An average horse can carry about twenty percent of its own body weight. Justice is sixteen hands and weighs a little over two thousand pounds. So, as long as we weigh less than four hundred together, we're good to go. Add to that, Justice is not an *average* horse—"

"Obviously," she interjected. "He's quite magnificent."

"Don't let him hear you... Flattery makes him insuffer-able," Hudson teased.

"Like owner, like horse, one might wonder," she sassed right back.

"Careful... Or you'll find yourself in a precarious situation."

"I thought you said I could trust you." Her voice was breathy.

"No, I never said that. I simply asked if you *do* trust me."

"My mistake."

Hudson was one thousand percent sure their ride — in fact, the entire morning — was *his* mistake...lock, stock, and barrel.

The warmth of her in the cage of his embrace, the sensa-tion of sheltering her body with his own, and her sweet, floral scent would haunt Hudson for a long time to come.

*Might as well make the torture worth the pain.*

"Hold on," he whispered in her ear. She rewarded him with a shiver.

It encouraged Hudson to show Ms. Blake Fisher what constituted going *so fast*.

Guiding them out of the woods and into a clearing of gentle slopes and smooth winter rye, Hudson let Justice run like the wind.

Hudson felt bruises forming from her vise grip on the arm he'd left wrapped around her ribs. But she never asked him to slow down, never showed fear, and never shied away from the glory of the horse's strength and power.

Just the opposite: Blake squealed with delight.

She lifted her face to the sun and the breeze. Her expres-sion displayed rapture and exhilaration. It might've been her first ride, but he'd put money on it not being her last.

When they neared another copse of trees leading into denser woods, Hudson slowed Justice to a canter, then a trot, and finally, a casual walk. Before they entered the shaded area, Blake leaned her head against his shoulder, closed her eyes to the sun, and basked in its glory.

Her radiant exhilaration bewitched him... A core element shifted deep in Hudson's soul.

"Thank you," she breathed.

## 7

### Might
*Auxiliary verb ~*
*Used to say something is possible.*

*W*ithout the sun's rays, the temperature dropped significantly. Blake opened her eyes to see where he'd led them.

"Oh wow," she exhaled in awe as Hudson dismounted Justice and tied his reins to a branch. "This is gorgeous."

"Welcome to Juniper Farm," Hudson said, reaching up to help her down from the saddle.

"This is the Christmas tree lot?" Blake marveled, setting her hands on his shoulders.

They were tight with muscle. She tried not to notice.

She also strove to ignore the electricity sparking between their bodies as his large hands tightened around her waist and ribs to lift her from the saddle. The charge intensified as his powerful arms held her close while he lowered her feet to the ground.

"A bit more than a tree lot, don't you think?" Hudson's low voice was understated.

"Yes," she agreed, walking from one beautiful big tree to another. "Hudson, it's incredible."

When he didn't reply, she looked back over her shoulder. He squinted back at her with his head tilted.

"What?" Blake wondered.

"You called me Hudson."

"I'd say we're past Mr. Sharp and Ms. Fisher, wouldn't you?"

Their morning had taken quite a detour.

"Yes — *Blake* — that's a fair assessment." He walked closer in long, efficient strides, his boots soundless on the earthen floor. Blake gulped but stood her ground. She experienced a flashback of their standoff the day before. So similar, yet so totally different.

"Come on." He held out a hand, a challenging gleam in his eyes as he waited to see if she'd take it.

*I might be a fool, but I'm not a coward.*

Palm to palm and fingers entwined, they stepped deeper into the forest.

They walked in silence, although the woods, filled with sounds and scents, prevented the moment from feeling awkward. Mesmerized by the variations of trees, Blake ran her fingertips along the bark of some. She'd snag a few leaves, a cluster of berries, or a bough of needles, holding them to her nose to inhale the spicy evergreen, so verdant and fresh, before tossing them to the forest floor.

Almost to another clearing, Hudson stopped walking. He dropped her hand and stood directly in front of her, arms crossed and knees bent until they were eye to eye. "So, what would you say we are?" he asked, picking up the conversation where it had left off several minutes earlier. "Friends? Enemies?"

"I don't want to be your enemy," Blake admitted, equally shocked by that truth and the forlorn tone it gave her voice.

"I'm not sure I can be your friend." His declaration hurt, like he'd stabbed a sharp horse pick into her heart. She nodded, intending to move away from him; she needed space to breathe. Lifting her chin, Hudson forced her to meet his gaze. "Because you want to take this — *this* — away from me." He looked around at the trees surrounding them, forcing her to follow the path of his gaze.

Regrasping her hand, he walked toward the clearing. She lagged, but he didn't release his hold. Once he'd essentially dragged her through the trees, she saw exactly where they were. The Wimberly Glass Factory.

Blake couldn't believe how close the abandoned business property sat to Twin Oaks. Of course, she'd seen the land, the pipe fence along the highway, the neglected gravel parking lot, the burnt-out warehouse, and the dilapidated showroom. But she'd never seen it from the Sharps' perspective.

"Did this area used to look like your land?" What a shame if he answered *yes*. What a travesty if the dried, deserted acreage had once been lush and fertile.

"At one point, I'm sure it looked like the natural areas we've never cleared. But not like the Christmas tree farm; that's one of a kind. Junior — my grandpa — gifted thirty acres to my Aunt Juni — Juniper — for her thirtieth birthday. She tossed thirty bags of tree seeds — juniper, of course, along with every other type of Christmas seedling she could get her hands on — across her acreage."

He shook his head in disbelief and chuckled as he continued, "Some of us spent the better part of a decade getting educated on the best ways to plan and plant fields, rotate crops, test soil, minimize stock and wildlife impacts on the land, and prioritize water access to ensure a decent yield and harvest. Not my Loony Aunt Juni." He said it with reverent dismay.

"She twirled in circles, chanting and singing, letting the seeds fly from her hands. She ran through the hills like a banshee, throwing handfuls of seedlings in the wind. When she realized just how much square footage thirty acres covers, she tossed seeds out the window of an old ranch truck. She never once considered how she'd irrigate the trees, never worried how to combat disease or pests."

"And this is what grew? Organically...naturally?"

"Yep," Hudson mocked, but with a genuine smile. "Call it divine intervention or beginner's luck. Whatever you call it, it's a miracle."

"Meant to be," Blake said to herself.

"Indeed," Hudson agreed.

Blake hadn't meant to say that out loud; she didn't need Hudson Sharp reading her mind.

"Perhaps it was meant to be here to bring peace and joy to others," Blake countered. "Couldn't you share just a small slice of the blessing?" She offered the compromise in earnest, and Blake hoped he saw she meant it when he studied her countenance for signs of artifice.

There were none. Both parties could win; Blake had bet her life on it...at least her life and career in Green Hills.

"You truly believe a revolving door of visitors will respect the land the same way my family has for the past hundred and forty years?"

"No, not the same," she answered honestly, backing up because he moved closer with each word she spoke. "But respect it? Yes, I do." She put her foot down, figuratively and literally, looking him right in the eyes.

"And you don't expect they'll ever litter, or chase away animals in their natural habit, which is now invaded, or carve names in the trees, or climb limbs not mature enough to hold the weight, or—"

"Okay," she interrupted to halt his argument, which was

building steam in direct proportion to his ire. He'd also advanced on her until her back flattened against the trunk of a large spruce. Nowhere else to go. Might as well face the fire.

"I get it," she said. "You've meticulously thought through every bad thing that could possibly happen. And you're right, they could. All those things *could* occur.

"But you know what else might happen?" she countered, bravely poking him in the chest and gearing up to hammer home each of *her* very compelling, very brilliant points. "Children *might* run through the woods, chasing squirrels and birds and siblings and friends, instead of hunkering down indoors. Families *might* spend a fabulous afternoon together, picnicking on the grounds, having an annual family portrait made for the holidays, and cutting down the perfect tree to decorate in their home, instead of ignoring one another, focused on computers and phones every second they're not at school or work. The community *might* gather here to sing carols, drink apple cider and hot chocolate, and collect donations for others in need, instead of keeping to themselves behind closed doors. Married couples *might* enjoy a date night, cuddling close to ward off the chill, sharing their day, their struggles, their worries, and their praises — truly hearing one another for the first time in years. Young lovers *might* wander through the trails, listening to one another's hopes and dreams while getting to know one another without the roar of a crowded restaurant, without the limitations of *not* talking during a movie, or without having to chat over a loud band in the background at Scooter's."

Hudson waited in silence for a full minute, probably in hopes Blake had finished her tirade.

When she refrained from speaking, he raised a hand — palm out — to serve as a shield over his heart, where she'd repeatedly — some might say *aggressively* — jabbed him. Six times.

*B*lake realized her tactical error the moment his husky voice purred its next words…

"I wonder if the young lovers will sneak away to find a special tree to claim as *theirs*," Hudson added to her list. Then he placed his other palm flat against the tree he'd backed her into, trapping her between the solid, unyielding trunk and his solid, unyielding strength. Hudson's speech grew heavier, sexier. Blake's pulse quickened.

"Maybe they'll hold hands," he continued in that thicker-than-molasses voice. To illustrate, Hudson slid the hand protecting his heart over her hand, entwining their fingers and curling their joined fists between them as he stepped even nearer. He raised an eyebrow, as if his wasn't the absolute craziest of ideas. Blake swore a flock of butterflies took flight in her stomach.

"They *might* even indulge in a kiss." Hudson's eyes darted to Blake's mouth. Her lips tingled beneath his gaze, to the point she had to moisten them.

Hudson might've growled.

Blake might've purred.

Blood rushed to her head, which had gone foggy and dazed. All the chirps and rustles of the woods faded from her ears. She and Hudson might've been the only two people on Earth. He filled her senses that much.

Hudson lifted his palm from the tree, and using the back of his hand, his fingers traced the line from her temple to her chin. Sliding his palm along her jawline, he cradled her cheek. His eyes scrutinized Blake like she was the most interesting puzzle he'd ever encountered. No one had ever looked at her that way.

His thumb swept across her bottom lip. Finally, his gaze — filled with an unspoken question — met her own.

"Yes." Her voice came out as little more than a whisper. Stronger than she sounded, Blake took the reins by sliding her hands across his collarbones and over his shoulders until her fingers tangled in the short hair at the back of his head. Rising onto the toes of her boots, she guided him to meet her halfway, his lips hovering mere millimeters from hers when she added, "They *might*."

## 8

*Mistakes are a fact of life.*
*It is the response to error that counts.*
**Nikki Giovanni**

Testing the softness of her skin, Hudson lambasted himself.

*You're an idiot… This is a mistake… What are you thinking?*

Studying her features, he memorized each freckle on her velvet skin. His nana used to call them Angel Kisses. The memory cloaked him in peace, silenced the deafening doubts.

*Is this woman heaven-sent to save me? And if so, from what? Or is she an agent of the devil, on a mission to lead me down a path of ruin?*

When their lips finally touched, all thoughts and doubts and questions disappeared.

Determined to let Blake take the lead, Hudson fought his knee-jerk reaction to pounce on her. Feet planted on the ground, he stood as solid and unmoving as the trees towering over them. When Blake untangled her fingers from his hair and wrapped her arms around his neck, Hudson gradually took over the discovery of their kiss.

Hudson tightened his arms around her ribs, drawing her closer and closer, until she no longer leaned against the spruce behind her, until he was all she touched.

Taking his fill of her warm and pliant lips, savoring the faint peachy taste of her lip gloss, Hudson branded the impression of their first kiss onto his brain.

It might be an irreversible mistake, but Hudson didn't want to forget it.

As if he could.

The way Blake Fisher fit in the envelope of his embrace, the way she gave as much as she took — the rightness of it all — was knowledge that, once known, could never be unknown.

A shiver passed through Blake. Whether it stemmed from desire or the air temperature, which had taken a dive to downright cold, Hudson didn't know, but it did get his attention. They needed to go back to the ranch.

And Hudson needed to gain some perspective on their morning; he couldn't ignore a nagging desire to dissect the turmoil roiling through him, a desire not quite but pretty close to being as strong as the urge to keep on kissing Ms. Fisher — indefinitely.

Slowing their ardor, Hudson loosened the cage of his arms. He eased back, but he didn't release her. Blake's arms slid from his shoulders as her heels returned to the earth beneath them. Still, they kissed.

By sheer strength of will, Hudson transformed their earth-shaking, soul-stealing connection into light, almost playful nips. When he lifted his lips from hers and looked into her eyes, the haze of longing clear in their fathomless depths nearly buckled his knees.

"Ohh," she sighed.

Framing her face with his hands, he glanced at her lips — swollen and glistening. He'd taken punches to the gut with much less impact than the sight of her dazed and flushed after they'd essentially devoured one another.

Maybe just one more taste?

*E*ventually, Hudson managed to stop kissing Blake, but doing so had been a task of epic proportions.

He'd never claimed to be a saint; he'd kissed his fair share of ladies. But he'd never experienced a kiss like that. He'd never encountered a woman like her.

Hudson had known it the moment they met: Blake Fisher was a force to be reckoned with.

She'd be a storm that wreaked all kinds of havoc.

That kiss— Those kisses — plural — were the stuff of fantasies, but they also represented a huge misstep, an error in judgment, that no doubt would come back to haunt him... most likely every single night when Hudson closed his eyes to sleep.

Yet, they were mistakes he didn't regret.

Riding Justice to the barn, with Blake in the saddle in front of Hudson as they'd ridden before, he admitted to himself: he wouldn't take it back, wouldn't undo their morning together, even if he could've reversed time.

"I thought you were a man," Hudson confessed, when neither of them had spoken since mounting the horse.

"Excuse me?" she asked, defaulting to what he'd discovered was her favorite response, not haughtily for once, but rather as if she'd been lost in thought.

"When I first received your letters and emails, I thought Blake Fisher was male."

"That happens," she told him. "With a first name tradition- ally given to boys and a vocational last name, I suppose it's easy to mistake me for a man. When did you figure it out?"

Rocking with the cadence of Justice's ambling walk, Blake relaxed against Hudson's chest. She was the picture of casual indifference. Hudson hoped her nerves strummed under the surface, just as his continued to do.

"Your voice — all honey and whiskey — filling up my voicemail," he teased. "Where's your accent from?"

"Alabama," she answered.

"Really? I went to school at Auburn University."

"Yes, I saw the gallery of diplomas and certificates in your office. War Eagle," she said.

"War Eagle," he replied, curious why her tone had changed when she mentioned his degrees.

Blake fell silent, but Hudson wanted to know more. He guided Justice the long way home to make the ride a little longer. Hudson didn't regret that decision, either.

"When did you move to Oklahoma? What brought you here?" he asked, when she'd not spoken in several minutes.

"My career," she explained. "Two and a half years ago, I took a job managing a real estate office in Oklahoma City. The job didn't work out, but during my time there, I realized I wanted to run my own company, to do things my way rather than at the whim of someone else."

"That makes sense. But why didn't the job work out?" Hudson had a feeling there was more to it than she'd let on.

"A difference of opinion with the owner, which led to an abuse of power, which led to an unfortunate incident. It was either make a scene, legally and politically, or remove myself from an ugly situation. I chose the latter."

"What happened?" Hudson wanted to know, suspecting someone had threatened her or hurt her in some way. It didn't sit well with him.

"I'd rather not get into the sordid details. It's enough that I got away. More than enough that I'm here now."

A thread of hope had Hudson wishing she meant here as

in surrounded by his strength and protection. More than likely, she meant here as in living and working in Green Hills.

He considered the difference, and what it meant that he wanted her to want to be with him.

So many opposing forces and feelings. Life sure could move to "complicated" status in a hurry.

"So why Green Hills?" he asked as the barns came into sight. "Our real estate market is slow and stable. Surely, working in OKC or Tulsa would be considerably more profitable, with a lot higher inventory and population growth."

"That's true, but I'm not in the market for a position on a hamster wheel. The rat race doesn't look appealing. I don't need to make millions, just enough to live comfortably, with a roof over my head, groceries in my kitchen, and a soft pillow on my bed. And I'd like to earn that by taking the time to get to know my clients... be part of a community. Maybe even find friends, feel connected."

"You chose well. Green Hills definitely fits that bill."

"Yes, I've seen that since the day I arrived. My business is just down from the square. I met Maree Davenport less than a minute after stepping from my car. Maree introduced me to Sadie Jones, to other members of her family, to friends she's made since moving to Green Hills about a year before I got here. They're wonderful."

Hudson stopped Justice outside the barn, looped his reins over a wooden hitching post, and moved to help her down.

Again, the air crackled as her body slid down his on her way back to earth.

"Of course, I'd been to Green Hills once before, so I knew what to expect," Blake added. "In fact, I met you back then... in a way."

Talk about dropping a bomb.

Hudson's eyes darted to hers. He studied her expression. Unreadable.

*B*efore Hudson could barrage Blake with questions, angle for information, or dig for more details, the triplets charged from the barn, kicking up dust and creating ear-splitting noise... a three-piece tornadic superstorm like always.

"You're back!" Bennie exclaimed.

"We heard Bennie almost killed everyone," Karl, ever the drama king, overexaggerated.

Bennie wrestled Karl in a pseudo tackle. Tobi took advantage of their chaos to sidle up to Blake.

"Seriously, are you okay?" he asked, far more flirtatiously than concerned.

"She's fine. We didn't almost die," Hudson pointed out, intercepting Tobi's attempt to whisk Blake away by stepping between them, "and I'm glad y'all are here."

That got the boys' attention.

"Justice needs to be brushed and bathed after y'all take off his saddle and tack. Then let him out with Topper, Ethel, and Lucy in the paddock before the snow arrives this afternoon. Be sure you add a little extra feed for Justice; he earned it this morning." With those instructions — commands, some might call them — Hudson grabbed Blake's hand and walked toward the Big House, with her literally in tow.

He didn't look back to see if the boys gawked or if Blake balked.

Hudson had questions — some he intended to ask her, and others he needed to decipher for himself.

And he would uncover the answers he sought.

## 9

*Humankind has not woven the web of life.*
*We are but one thread within it.*
*Whatever we do to the web, we do to ourselves.*
*All things are bound together.*
*All things connect.*
*Attributed to Chief Seattle,*
*Duwamish Tribe of the Northwest,*
*from a speech given in the*
*Lushootseed dialect, c. 1854,*
*Translated into English by*
*Doctor Henry A. Smith*
*and published in the*
*Seattle Star, October 29, 1887*

*H*udson dragged Blake through the back door, past the kitchen, across the main hallway, and into his office. He deposited her onto the middle cushion of a massive, overstuffed saddle brown leather sofa in front of a monstrous fireplace, where perfectly tended flames danced and crackled and filled the room with a warm, welcoming glow and the resinous scent of burning logs.

"Stay," he commanded, with a look that expressed his expectation of her obedience, then left the room with curt steps.

Tempted to leave just to prove she could, Blake huffed in response. But instead of taking off, she satisfied her need to *not* be sitting on the couch when he returned by roaming the room, taking in book titles, family photos, and artwork the likes of which she'd never seen.

The collection rivaled anything she could've imagined: Bronze sculptures and ceramic figurines of animals, cowboys, and nature added depth and color to the shelves and tables. Framed canvases included oil paintings, watercolors, and acrylics of all sizes. A stunning wool blanket, heavy and thick, hung on a wall, an incredible piece of Native American art. And the books! An obsessive reader, Blake could've gotten lost in the endless stacks of books that lined every wall, nearly floor to ceiling.

She stood on the far side of the room, looking at a smaller but fascinating painting, when Hudson walked back through the ornately carved double doors of his office. His features went dark when he first looked at the empty sofa. His lips flattened into a grim line, and his jaw twitched.

"Is this the actual deed to Twin Oaks?" she asked, alerting him she hadn't left, before he could blow a gasket in irritation.

His gaze snapped to hers, and she'd have sworn relief washed over his face.

Continuing into the room, he closed — and locked — the doors. Then he hung his heavy canvas winter vest and brown felt cowboy hat on a rack.

"Yes," he finally answered, joining her in front of the picture frame. "Please don't steal it."

Blake turned a sour frown on him. Hudson simply lifted

one eyebrow.

*Harrumph.*

Hudson almost grinned at her growl. Then he faced the embellished deed.

"My great-great-great-granddad, Tobias Karl Benjamin von Sharp, followed Captain David L. Payne to Oklahoma in 1881. Payne, considered a brilliant linguist in his time, spoke several languages and served as a key negotiator with the Indian Nations and tribal leaders. Tobias von Sharp ventured this way with Captain Payne in a group of German immigrants. According to diaries and letters, when Tobias set eyes on the twin oaks, small and immature as new trees all begin, but perfectly placed where God set them atop a wide rise in the green hills, he knew he'd found his home."

"Your parents named the triplets after him, your grandpa three times removed? That's one way to keep the legends alive."

"It's out of respect, and yes, to keep the family history at the forefront." He spoke in a serious tone. She'd meant the comment to be lighthearted, but there was no teasing with Hudson where the ranch was concerned.

"This land is timeless," he continued. "It's more than one person, more than the seven generations we've lived here. We're temporary, but Twin Oaks is forever."

His steely voice motivated Blake to change the subject; otherwise, they'd be arguing about the teeny-tiny sliver of Twin Oaks she needed him to sell, and in no time flat.

"And this is the deed to it? Just hanging on the wall? Forever?"

She leaned in to read the elegant, flowing script behind the scene of cattle painted on the document. Both the nineteenth-century handwriting in faded ink and the modern brushstrokes in vivid acrylics astounded Blake, each stoutly strong yet reverently beautiful.

"The Homestead Act of 1862 made it legal for a settler to claim a hundred sixty acres of public land, and if they survived on it for five years, they'd earn the title to that land. Tobias didn't like the idea of stealing from the tribes that lived around this part of the country; he didn't think his young bride back on the East Coast would feel safe joining him here if the settlers were at odds with the Native Americans."

"That's quite the understatement, isn't it?"

"Yes, I'm sure it is. And I'm also sure what we read in history books, written with an agenda and an angle, doesn't scratch the surface of the atrocities of that time." Hudson paused, pain and regret on his face — sadness for actions and wrongs done more than a hundred years before he'd been born. Blake didn't doubt his sincerity. It was plain to see the wounds of the land were part of his soul. "Tobias wouldn't do it," Hudson stated with pride. "He forced Payne to act as interpreter and brokered a deal with the local tribes. With a combination of cash, bartering, and contracts for future partnerships, Tobias bought his hundred and sixty acres."

"I didn't know people did that — worked *with* the Indians," Blake marveled.

"I'd imagine they were few and far between," Hudson agreed. "But each time a settler gave up on surviving on their land, Tobias, his son Otto, and every Sharp since paid a fair price to add the acreage to Twin Oaks."

"How big is the ranch now?" she asked.

"*Really* big."

Blake harrumphed again, not impressed with that answer.

Hudson shook his head at her and trudged on through his explanation of the unique piece of art she'd asked about.

"Anyway, to have some sort of official paperwork recording the sale — even though Payne argued it wasn't legit until Tobias's five years were up — they wrote out this deed, and everyone present at the negotiation signed it. Once Tobias received his formal deed from the United States government, that became the official document, and this one lived securely in a tattered ledger book for decades. Mom came across it a few years ago and commissioned someone who specializes in document art to paint a scene from the ranch on it. Before he painted it, he copied and preserved the document, and the glass is airtight as well as fade-resistant to protect it. *Forever.*"

"It's incredible. I'm guessing you have all kinds of historically amazing artifacts around here," she said, ignoring his *forever* exclamation and walking to another dark wooden frame. Under the glass, a swath of tanned hide affixed to a grasscloth mat showed off an intricate drawing of a warrior with his horse. "How old is this?"

"*Really* old," he answered with a grin. "Come here. I have questions for you to answer."

Blake angled a look at him, again unimpressed by his dodging tactics, but she followed him to the sitting area where he'd originally left her. She sat in the same spot as before. He crouched in front of the fireplace and stoked the fire with an iron poker. When he'd added another two logs and adjusted them to his liking, Hudson walked to his desk, where he tossed a pair of well-worn buttery yellow leather work gloves onto a stack of file folders. He walked back to stare at the fire for a long moment and *finally* took a seat on the heavy plank coffee table, which separated the couch from the hearth. He faced Blake, elbows on knees, and hands clasped between them. His relaxed posture belied the tic of his clenched jaw.

"What do you mean, *We met back then...* In what way?" Hudson asked. "For better or worse, I'm positive I'd remember meeting you."

His grimacing frown was almost comical. He wanted to hate her — Blake could sense it. But hard as he might try, she didn't think he actually could. No, she'd have wagered he was just as drawn to her as she was to him since the day they met...

## 10

*Childhood is the one story*
*that stands by itself in every soul.*
**Ivan Doig**

*Summer 2006 ~ Daisy Lake, Green Hills, Oklahoma*

"*D*on't walk too close," the Bimbo Barbie wannabe sneered. "She'll give you lice." The blond girl had perfect skin, tanned to a perfect bronze, and a perfect body, barely covered by a blue gingham bikini.

Blake had admired the girl's beauty from afar all day, watching her laugh with carefree abandon as her friends flocked around her, and wishing for the confidence to join their beach volleyball game or even speak to the teenagers. She'd tried to look away when the cutest boy draped an arm over the girl's shoulders and steered her toward a small rowboat, held her hand when she stepped inside, and then rowed her the short distance to a shaded inlet where they kissed and giggled and flirted. Blake had experienced pure stomach-churning jealousy watching those kids swim and splash and goof off in the sparkling lake. She'd wanted it all.

By force of will — already strong and sadly necessary for the thirteen-year-old — Blake had tamped down her envy, channeling that energy into daydreaming about the day she'd be the one with shiny waves of long hair, a stylish swimsuit, and a doting gentleman holding out a hand to help her. Someday, she'd be the one people spoke to, rather than about. She'd have the shiny convertible, the pristine white tailored shorts and freshly pressed blue blouse over her pricey two-piece, and the fun cork-wedge high heel sandals that accentuated toned calves and long, lean legs. She'd stay in one of the quaint, homey cabins beside Daisy Lake, barbecue chicken on the open grill, and serve copious amounts of sides, salads, and sweet desserts on fun and lively printed platters and colorful coordinating bowls, made from that hard plastic Mama had told her about after washing dishes in The Lodge's restaurant. Mela-*something*, Blake recalled.

She could see it all so clearly in her head that she'd become lost in her vision and not noticed the teenagers meander by her perch on a boulder between the lodge and the beach. The hateful, snide remark woke her from her musings.

Instead of tossing the barb and walking on, the beautiful girl stopped to stare at Blake.

"When was the last time you bathed? Or washed that rat's nest? I mean, it looks like you have a dirty mop on your head."

The girl — obviously pretty on the outside only — exaggerated. The whole reason Mama had taken the summer job at The Lodge at Daisy Lake was because they could camp on the grounds for free while she cooked and cleaned in the kitchen, which meant unlimited access to the lake, allowing for daily baths. Blake had washed her body and shampooed her hair just hours earlier. The rat's nest part wasn't true either; Blake's Mama was a magician with braids, and she'd created a fabulous style for Blake before heading to work, beginning at the base of her hairline and braiding up to the crown of her head, where the plait ended in a thick ponytail of long auburn waves. Her clothes might be threadbare, and her shoes might have come apart at the sole, but Blake knew her hair did *not* look dirty. In fact, it was the one facet of her appearance she could confidently say looked good.

But Blake said nothing.

Snooty, spiteful comments weren't anything new. Blake had discovered years before that the best course of action in such a situation was no action. She'd tried being hateful back, but while that never seemed to have any effect on the person being tacky, Blake always walked away feeling bad, frustrated with herself that they had pulled her down to their level of hatred. She'd also found that reasoning was a waste of her breath; ugly people enjoyed being that way; they didn't want to have their mind changed, so no matter how much sense she made, they'd never alter their outlook or see things through Blake's eyes.

Mean girls — and boys — existed everywhere Blake and Mama had gone, and they'd gone to lots of places. Each town, each church, and each school Blake had ever stepped foot in contained a bully or two. Blake had resigned herself to their presence. She'd developed thick skin and a deaf ear.

The beauty queen at Daisy Lake wasn't new, she wasn't unique, and she wasn't special.

She was, however, just warming up.

Apparently content with an easy target for her venom, the girl called out to her friends, telling them they had to see the specimen she'd found by the beach...a living, breathing troll, with frizzy hair, dirty clothes, and a fat face.

Again with the hair! The girl had imagined the other two accusations as well. Mama's philosophy that no matter how little they had, they could always find soap and water meant that in addition to daily baths, clothes got a good scrubbing every night. And while Blake certainly didn't have sunken cheeks, with food supplies scarce, she was a far cry from pudgy or plump, and miles away from fat.

In fact, after her pretty hair, Blake kind of liked her figure. Mama said she still had some blooming to do, but that Blake was blossoming *just right, and in God's timing.* Eye to eye with her mom, Blake had reached five feet, six inches tall. Hours and hours practicing with the middle school track team had created lean muscles on her long legs. Swimming in Daisy Lake every allowable minute throughout the summer had toned and strengthened her shoulders, arms, and abs, too.

That blond socialite must've been crazy. Surely so if she considered Blake's stature fat. Blake opened her mouth to express just that opinion when the gorgeous guy from the beach and the rowboat jogged over per his girlfriend's summoning.

"Con, let's go," he urged. He spared Blake a glance, but he didn't seem to notice her shoddy thrift store shirt. Instead, his expression apologized for the mean girl and her suddenly present entourage.

"But, Hudson — just look at her," the girl said in a whiny voice, while pointing at Blake with a wriggling finger, as though Blake was a leech.

"Constance," he said firmly, but she didn't retreat.

"Lake trash," one of their female friends scoffed. "You'd think the lodge would run 'em off so they don't scare away the good people."

"I don't know," a boy beside her said. "I'm sure she'd be good for something." He left no doubt as to the only activity he thought she'd be *good for.*

Unease crept into Blake's stomach. The rich kids outnumbered her a dozen to one. If they wanted to cause trouble — real trouble — she'd be hard-pressed to fight them off.

"Eww," the girl — Constance — gagged. "You'd have to clean her before you touched her. Especially before you—"

"That's enough," a strong, commanding voice cut her off. Hudson, the girl had called him. What a unique name. It matched his green eyes, which switched between the color of Christmas trees and emerald jewels, unlike anything Blake had ever seen.

"Come on, Hud. We're just having fun," the disgusting boy teased, reaching out to tousle Blake's ponytail.

In her panicked haste to dodge his hand, Blake slipped on the boulder. When she fell, her face hit the huge rock. A broken stick, jutting from a crack in the stone, jabbed and tore the soft skin along the top of her lip. Blood immediately gushed from the cut.

"Yuck," Constance eeked. "I guess now we know gutter rats bleed red."

Having spewed the last word, she flounced away, her posse close on her heels.

Except for Hudson.

He reached toward Blake to grasp her upper arm and help her up. But Blake skittered back to protect herself.

"I'm not going to hurt you," he said. The light reflected like diamonds in his eyes, like sun glistening off droplets of green grass after a summer rain. "I promise," he added with a kind smile. "Let's get you inside to stop the bleeding and see if you need stitches."

"I can't go in The Lodge," Blake replied. "If the kitchen manager sees me like this, or if he thinks I've made trouble, they'll fire Mama."

"That's ridiculous. This wasn't your fault. At all."

"That won't matter," she told him. "It's fine. *I'm* fine. It'll stop bleeding in a minute." She looked around for cloth or something to hold against her lip, which burned like fire. Her eyes scanned the ground around them, but Blake didn't see a towel or rag, so she walked toward the water to rinse it in the lake.

"No, don't do that. The lake water isn't good for it." Hudson jogged to stop her. "I've got water bottles in my truck; come on."

The blood, thickening but not stopping its flow, must've been a rough sight, because Hudson pulled his t-shirt over his head, shook out the sand and dirt, and folded it into a tight ball. Then he held it to her mouth with kind gentleness.

Flustered by Hudson and his gesture — or possibly by the tight muscles across his chest and the perfect six-pack across his stomach — Blake held the shirt to catch the blood and shooed his hand away.

He just smiled down at her with that twinkle in his eyes. Then he grasped her free hand and pulled her toward the boat ramp and parking lot.

When they reached a huge white four-door pickup truck, he pulled a key from his swim shorts and hit a button to unlock the doors as well as the tailgate. He grabbed a few fluffy striped beach towels from the back seat, a first aid kit in a red plastic box, and a blue cooler from the floorboard. Tucking the supplies under one arm and switching the cooler to that hand, he closed the truck door and took Blake's hand in his free one.

He led them to the back of the truck, dropped her hand to open the tailgate, and set everything down. Then, as if she were no bigger than a child, Hudson hoisted her to sit on the lowered tailgate.

Her stomach did a flippy-floppy thing, which felt a lot like nausea, but not quite to the point of puking.

Hudson eased the bloody shirt from her wound and rotated it until he found a clean, dry area. With clenched hands, he made to rip it.

"No!" Blake gasped. "Don't tear it; it's a perfectly good shirt."

"It's okay," he reassured her. "I have plenty." He said it with such a confident smile, Blake didn't argue when he proceeded to shred the nice tee. What a waste. "See?" He dashed to the passenger side of the truck and snagged two more t-shirts. He shrugged into one — more's the pity — and set the other on the tailgate next to Blake.

"What's that for?" she questioned.

"Your shirt is covered in blood, and I'm sure you don't want to go around in just your swim top the rest of the day. It'll be too big, but it's super soft."

Again with the dazzling smile.

What was it like to be that confident, that sure? Looking at the fancy truck, with the luxurious leather interior, sprayed-on bed liner, and tinted windows, he'd clearly never known anything *but* self-assurance.

Hudson shifted so his back faced Blake while he opened the cooler and grabbed a bottle of water and two sodas. She figured he'd moved to give her a modicum of privacy to switch shirts. She could've explained that in her lifeguardesque one-piece tank-style swimsuit, she had nothing to hide. But again, his gesture spoke of thoughtfulness.

"Okay," she said, cramming her old shirt under her leg and picking up the new one. She inhaled deeply as she pulled the cotton knit over her face. It smelled like fresh laundry, new leather from his truck, and him. "Thanks," she added, hoping to sound grateful.

In reality, she was confused.

Blake had seen Hudson and his set owning the lake, The Lodge, and the beach all summer. They arrived most days just after lunch and played around all afternoon — swimming and lounging on the beach and the dock, rowing paddleboards or racing Jet Skis, fishing or riding in their boats. Until that day, Blake had avoided their notice, but she'd seen them. They lived a charmed life, in an exclusive rich-kid bubble. Clearly, they didn't need or desire to know anyone else.

So, why the nice-guy act?

"This might sting," Hudson told her. "Sorry." He grimaced as he laid a cotton ball drenched in hydrogen peroxide against her wounded skin. The sharp burning sensation in her lip brought tears to her eyes. "I think you could use a couple of stitches, but if you're adamant about not going inside to tell someone what happened, I have a butterfly bandage in here that might work."

"Thank you," Blake whispered through clenched teeth and around the seething cotton ball. She refused to let those tears fall, or to show any kind of weakness in front of Hudson.

"I'm sorry," he said again.

"What for?" she mumbled while he cleaned the deep cut.

"For them, for what they said. For you getting hurt."

Did he mean physically or emotionally? The two were entirely different types of pain.

"It's nothing I haven't heard before, and it doesn't matter. Not one bit. People like that—"

"Shhh," he soothed, placing a finger on her lips to hold them in place while he pulled the slice shut with the bandage. His warm breath, so close. The heat of his touch, so...*much.* Blake's lungs struggled to fill.

"They're not worth your time," he continued as he trimmed the two ends of the first aid strip. "The best part of leaving Green Hills for college after my senior year will be meeting new people, people I haven't been stuck with since the day I was born." He fiddled with the bandage a little more, then doused another strip of clean t-shirt with water from a bottle. She sat still, watching the muscles ripple in his forearms as he wrung out the cotton, and tried not to flinch when he used the damp rag to clean blood and grime off her cheekbone, which had also hit the rock pretty hard when she stumbled and fell, causing a nasty scrape of skin.

"You've lived here your entire life?" she asked, curious what that felt like. She and Mama were practically nomadic, going wherever Mama found work to sustain them for a few months, a year at most.

"All seventeen years," he confirmed. "Although my family has been here since the beginning of Green Hills — even helped found it." Pride boomed in his voice.

"And what's the worst part of going to college?"

"Being away from Twin Oaks. That's our ranch, the one my ancestors started all those years ago. It's my favorite place on the planet." His tone revealed a tiny vulnerability. It surprised Blake that he allowed her to see it. "I'll give you this… When you do something, you really go after it," he said with wincing chagrin. "You took off several layers of skin. It's as clean as I can get it with water. Lay your head over; I want to pour the rest of the hydrogen peroxide over it."

Blake leaned on her right arm and tilted her ear toward her shoulder. Instead of pouring the antiseptic from the travel-sized bottle, Hudson splayed his left hand under her head like a pillow. With his free hand, he shoved the cooler back and piled the beach towels into a mound. "Here," he offered, guiding her to lie on her side across the tailgate, her head on the towels. "This'll be easier."

She followed his lead, shifting her hips and folding her arms into her chest as he gently laid her down. Blake could barely breathe, and the people on the lake could probably hear her swallow. She said a quick prayer that Hudson would assume her nerves were about the impending pain of cleaning the scrape.

Oddly, he didn't remove his left hand, the one supporting her head. She closed her eyes and focused on the feel of it, so warm against her face. Blake tried to memorize the sensation of his strong fingers threaded into her hair. And she concentrated on the rough texture of the calluses on his palm, sure signs he wasn't just a pretty boy at the lake, but someone willing to work.

"Sorry," he breathed when she tensed at the tingling burn of the chemical cleaning her raw wound. "Peroxide isn't supposed to sting, but then even water burns skin this torn." Then he leaned in and blew soft, cool air on her cheek to soothe it.

Blake opened her eyes to look into his face. So beautiful. Again, she strove to memorize every detail: his deep green eyes, and the long lashes and thick sun-bleached, light brown eyebrows that framed them; the tanned skin, perfect and unblemished; the short dark blond whiskers around his strong jawline, shining in the sunlight.

"Are you going to be a doctor?" she asked, hating to break the spell of the moment, but more afraid to let him walk away without knowing more about him.

"Nah," he chuckled. "I just have a lot of practice in first aid; between the ranch, rodeoing, and doing stupid stuff with my friends, I seem to need this kit for someone on a regular basis." His self-deprecating laugh didn't hide the fact that Hudson took care of others, that his confidence made him a natural leader.

Reaching back into the plastic box, he retrieved antibiotic ointment, a gauze pad, and some medical tape. Hudson wasn't lying; he had a full doctor's bag of junk in there. He dabbed the area around the scrape to be sure it was dry. Then he slid his left hand from under her head. Immediately, Blake missed his touch.

She remained as still as a statue while he applied the ointment, positioned the gauze, and tore a piece of white tape into two long, skinny strips to secure the bandage.

"That should keep the dirt out and help it heal."

Blake pushed herself upright.

"Thank you." How could she keep him talking to her — taking care of her — a little longer? Their few minutes together was the least lonely she'd felt in such a long time. "You didn't have to do all that, but I appreciate it."

"I should've stepped in sooner." A deep frown appeared; his eyes darkened to the color of rich, earthy moss. "I feel bad for letting them say as much as they did, for them treating you that way. I don't know why I stood there silent."

"You don't *let* people do mean things. You can't control their actions any more than you can control their words. Mama always says every person's behavior is their own doing — we can't do it for 'em. We can only do for ourselves."

"That's awful wise," he replied, the smile back in his eyes.

"Mama is wise. People don't think she is, 'cause she didn't go to college and doesn't have a fancy job. But she's smart. I know life's taught her some tough lessons, but she never gives up. She never takes the easy way out and never quits." Blake wasn't sure if someone like Hudson could understand what the easy way out and quitting meant, but Blake did. She, too, had learned a lot about the world.

"You're smart, too," Hudson told Blake. The genuine and forthright respect in his gaze embarrassed Blake. She didn't know how to respond, so she looked down at her bare feet, which were tanned but dirty. The unpolished nails looked nothing like the French pedicures and bright, summery colors Blake had seen on the toes of the girls Hudson had been with at the beach.

They came from — *belonged in* — two different worlds.

Blake hopped down from Hudson's tailgate.

She grabbed the hem of the t-shirt he'd loaned her to return it. Hudson stopped her by placing his hands on her wrists, lightly but firmly.

"No, you keep it." The lighter jadelike streaks of green in his eyes swirled like a distant storm.

Blake nodded her thanks, worried her voice would crack and tears would fall if she tried to say anything. Something about Hudson — or maybe the ordeal with his friends — had put her on-edge, made her emotions ping-pong all over the place.

She snatched her ruined shirt from the bed of the truck and walked away, before she made a fool of herself and without looking back.

## 11

*Circumstances may cause*
*interruptions and delays,*
*but never lose sight of your goal.*
**Mario Andretti**

*S* *he's the one.*

The realization had barely struck Hudson when banging erupted at his office doors.

"Go away," he roared, casting a glance at Blake before looking down at his boots. He resumed his pacing.

He'd accomplished maybe four trips in front of the fireplace when three faces appeared outside his window. He bestowed his grumpiest frown, but they didn't take the hint.

Having not grabbed their coats before traipsing through the cold and into the flower beds to get Hudson's attention, the triplets jumped up and down, rubbing their hands together while comically shaking and shivering.

"We're hungry," Tobi whined loudly.

"What's for lunch?" Karl asked.

Bennie grinned. "Is Blake staying?"

"Yes," Hudson thundered, with plenty of volume for all to hear, through the thick glass of the window and even though he faced toward the room and away from the boys.

"No — I'm not!" Blake exclaimed, popping up from the couch and heading for the office door.

"Yes, she is," Hudson reiterated. Then he turned back to the window and growled, "Get inside and set out sandwich stuff. We'll be there in a minute."

With long strides Hudson beat Blake to the door and blocked her way.

"I have to go," she stated.

"We have to talk." He placed his hands on her shoulders, forcing her to meet his gaze.

Blake couldn't stand the direct connection. Her eyes darted anywhere but at his face. "You wanted to know when we met. Now you know. And I need to leave." She tried to step around Hudson, but he didn't budge.

"Please," Hudson whispered, using his index finger to lift her chin. "Please stay. Just for lunch, just for a while."

*H*udson hadn't formed a plan for if she refused. Luckily, she acquiesced. True, she did so on a deflated sigh, but she'd agreed to join them for a bite of lunch, casual and comfortable, nonetheless.

Honestly, with the boys in attendance, she wouldn't have to say a word, so she had nothing to fear.

Hudson didn't care if she spoke or not; he just didn't want her to go. *That* was an issue he'd explore at a later time.

*S*he's the one.

For the rest of that summer, the one before his senior year of high school, Hudson had looked for the mystery girl all over Green Hills, everywhere he'd gone: around the high school, where he went to strength and conditioning work-outs each morning after his chores at the ranch; the beach volleyball courts, where he'd seen her before; The Lodge at Daisy Lake, where he'd thought her mom worked; downtown, where local kids liked to hang out to shop and eat and socialize; the Majestic movie theater, where teenagers went on dates in a small town with little for minors to do after dark; and even at church, where his family sat on the front pew every Sunday morning.

All to no avail. She'd disappeared.

He'd asked around, even asked his mom, which had opened a whole can of worms. But no one knew who she was, or where she'd gone.

Hudson hadn't even known her name.

Since then, anytime he saw someone of her stature, with the auburn brown waves of her hair, and her determined stride, his heart sped up. He'd jog to catch up with the person, but each time he walked away disappointed. Once, during a business trip to Denver, Colorado, he even called out to someone at the airport. He'd been so sure she was the girl. But all he'd accomplished was embarrassing himself and making the traveler's boyfriend angry.

He'd always kept one eye open for anyone resembling her.

He'd worried about her, wondered about her, and dreamed about her for years.

But why hadn't he recognized her standing right in front of him?

Needing a moment to process the revelation, Hudson

claimed he had a quick phone call to make before lunch. He pointed Blake toward the kitchen and returned to his desk.

Elbows perched on the desktop, his chin resting on clasped hands, Hudson stared at his computer screen, but didn't see a thing.

*She's the one.*

Those three words sifted through his mind on a continual loop.

Another layer of thoughts — questions, really — muddled with the discovery. Where had she gone that summer? Where had she lived? Had her mom lost her job because of the local kids causing trouble? Had she found another job somewhere else? Was that why Hudson never saw her again? What had Blake been doing the past fourteen years?

Of course, he knew part of that answer. She'd earned her real estate license, become a broker, and established a business in Green Hills, helping residents purchase homes, businesses... and land.

She wanted his land.

Reconciling the quiet girl from that summer with the spit-fire woman currently in his kitchen proved difficult.

No wonder Hudson hadn't seen it — hadn't seen *her*.

He'd been too busy seeing an enemy.

Hudson rubbed his hands over his face. *Now what?*

The quiet murmur of voices reached Hudson before he entered the large, nearly commercial kitchen.

He stopped in the hallway to listen, trying to figure out what the boys were talking about with Blake. Rarely had he heard the triplets hold a nice, normal conversation, one that didn't include whooping and hollering and shouting over one another. But there they were, chatting pleasantly with her.

Hudson couldn't decipher their words, and he didn't want to be caught eavesdropping, so he tiptoed a few feet back down the hall. Then he walked normally, boots clipping on the floor as usual, and joined them in the kitchen.

The sight before him stunned Hudson into silence.

The four of them stood around the big work island, all four wearing aprons.

Tobi was chopping an apple on a cutting board. Karl was peeling and dicing hard-boiled eggs into a small silver bowl. Bennie was setting handfuls of chips on five plates laid out before him. And Blake was mixing something in a bigger silver bowl.

Since when did the triplets help in the kitchen?

As he walked toward the island, a timer on the oven beeped.

"Oh good." Blake glanced his way. "You can take the cookies out of the oven."

"Y'all made cookies?" Hudson asked, a bit dumbfounded.

"We found a roll of chocolate chip dough in the fridge. So, to be fair, we only *baked* cookies," she retorted.

Hudson used a hot pad to pull the cookie sheet from the oven and set it on the cooktop. Then he asked, "What else can I do?" as he walked to her side.

"Tobi, Karl, and I are mixing tuna salad. Bennie's prepping the plates. You can get us all something to drink, if you don't mind." Blake smiled up at him without guile or games. She could've held a grudge, or been irritated that Hudson had strong-armed her to stay. Instead, Blake appeared to genuinely enjoy being in the kitchen with his brothers, doing something so mundane as making sandwiches for lunch.

She'd been right during their ride: he didn't know her at all.

## 12

*Do I not destroy my enemies
when I make them friends?
Commonly attributed to
Emperor Sigismund or
Abraham Lincoln*

Despite Hudson's objections otherwise, the triplets weren't nearly as bad as their reputation claimed. In fact, Blake had a ton of fun with them during lunch. She'd been an avid audience, hearing about college, listening to the ways COVID had disrupted their year, and learning about their true love: rodeoing.

Before she left, she and Bennie had planned her riding lessons for the two weeks leading up to Christmas. She'd also arranged a time to teach Karl how to make chocolate cream pies — with extra-tall meringue — before a holiday party he and his brothers wanted to attend. And she'd agreed to meet the boys at Scooter's Thursday night, to hear Tobi and his band play on open mic night.

Hudson had walked her to the barn, where her car had remained parked since she arrived that morning. He stood by her SUV while she unlocked the door, but when she pulled on the driver's side door, he laid a hand on it to hold it closed.

Blake looked up to see why he'd stopped her; the intensity of his gaze caused a flutter in her chest.

"I looked everywhere for you that summer. And every day since." Hudson's right hand lifted to cradle her jaw. His thumb slid over the scar just above her lip, feeling the marred skin. His eyes followed the tracing movement.

"Well, now you know where I am." She'd been going for witty, but the words came out breathy and inviting instead.

"True," he agreed, moving closer. "But now I have to decide what to do about it."

Then Hudson lowered his lips to Blake's. He brushed them across hers, nipping at her scar, and soothing it with another caring caress of his thumb.

His hands, large and strong, framed her face. His fingers delved into the mass and weight of her hair until the back of her neck tingled with their warmth.

Instinctively, Blake grabbed hold of his forearms. Whether to control the situation or simply holding on for dear life, she couldn't be sure.

The latter proved to be the case when Hudson deepened their kiss.

Somehow, they'd extricated themselves from one another.

Somehow, she'd driven herself home in one piece.

And somehow, Blake had continued on with her day, and her week, and her life.

Yet, that kiss stayed with her throughout every waking moment.

And she dreamed of it throughout every minute of sleep.

The cute boy who'd intrigued her with his kindness and awakened her with his good looks had grown into a man — a demanding, controlling, infuriating, magnetic, gorgeous man.

*Friday, December 18, 2020*

*A* week later, Blake stared out her car window, parked in front of her office on Pin Oak Lane, allowing Hudson Alexander Sharp — the Fourth — to consume her thoughts yet again. So lost in her remembrance of that last kiss, the shrill ringing of her cell phone just about caused a heart attack.

"Hello?" she said, after a brief and calming breath.

"I heard you're taking riding lessons at Twin Oaks," Maree Davenport replied cheerfully. "And killing it! That's so great, Blake. Bennie taught me to ride last summer, and I have to confess, there's nothing quite as exhilarating as galloping across the plains. Maybe we can start riding together when you finish your lessons."

"I'd like that," Blake agreed. Maree's bubbly nature rubbed off on everyone who came into contact with her. Based upon the sheer number of friends she'd made in Green Hills in the few years since she'd made it her home, one would never guess Maree — and the rest of the Davenports — hadn't lived in Green Hills their whole lives. "Maybe we should begin *after* the weather warms up a bit," Blake added. "I had a lesson this morning, and it was downright frigid out there."

"I also heard you've been corralling the Sharp triplets; that's quite a feat."

"They're tolerable…once you get past their enthusiastically

immature mindset of being young, invincible, and far too thrill-seeking," Blake joked. "Honestly, they're quite endearing; all three of them have enormous hearts and sweet, chivalrous personalities. The triplets are alike in some ways, yet wholly unique from one another in others. It's been fun getting to know them."

"And how about their big brother? Any progress there?" Maree asked.

Boy, if that wasn't a loaded question!

Blake had successfully avoided Hudson at all three of her riding lessons so far.

She'd not been so successful when they gathered at Scooter's the night before, listening to live music and supporting Tobi's band. But she had escaped the evening basically unscathed, if she didn't count being a complete jumble of nerves after Hudson commandeered her on the dance floor, where he wrapped her in his arms for the slowest slow dance she'd ever experienced.

True, even a day later, when she closed her eyes, her memory invoked the smell of his cologne, spicy and earthy and so very Hudson. She could still feel his heat, a comforting yet intoxicating warmth emanating from the firm muscles of his chest. And there was that moment, when the song ended, when Hudson hadn't let her go. When instead, he'd tucked her left hand against his heart, so his right hand was free to run his knuckles down her cheek…to stroke his index finger along her jawline…to caress her scar again with the pad of his thumb. And when his lips, soft and smooth, lightly — *too lightly*—

"Blake? Are you still there? Did I lose you?" Maree called out over the phone.

"Oh— Uh— Sorry. The line must've cut out for a second," Blake stuttered.

*Or my brain cells did.*

Indeed, if Maree bought that flimsy excuse, Blake had some oceanfront property in Arizona to sell her.

"It's probably this storm they say is headed our way. Speaking of that, I wanted to let you know I'm headed to Kansas City this afternoon, just in case the roads get bad overnight. So I won't see you at yoga tomorrow. It's the baby's first Christmas, and I'm champing at the bit to get to Max and Janie Lyn's. Rhys will drive up on Christmas Eve, but he'll be around until then if you need anything, okay?"

"Thanks," Blake responded, a small lump in her throat at the kindness and friendship Maree offered so freely. It exemplified what Blake loved most about Green Hills and defined why she wanted to stay so badly. "Please assure Janie Lyn I'm still working on Hudson Sharp to sell that little bit of acreage we need for The Christmas Collection. He's not making it easy, but I'm not giving up. By next Christmas, y'all will be up and running," she pledged. Come hell or high water, she'd see to it. "And give your precious nephew a snuggle for me; I'm jealous you'll be spending the next several days loving on him and indulging in that sweet baby smell."

"Oh yeah, I intend to spend hours and hours rocking and cuddling and not much of anything else," Maree confessed with a joyful giggle.

The girls visited for a while longer, catching up on Maree's work projects and brainstorming for their next girls' night, which was already scheduled for January, and when they ended the call, peace and confidence filled Blake.

She belonged in Green Hills. She'd found friends who cared for her. She'd established her place in the community. No one — not even Hudson Sharp — would take that away.

With renewed determination, she wrote another email to Sharp Enterprises, attached a new document outlining The Christmas Collection and the positive impact it undoubtedly would have on Green Hills, as well as the full business proposal the Davenport girls had created, and requested *another* time to meet to discuss a sales contract that benefited all parties involved.

Within seconds of Blake hitting the send button, he replied.

That was a first. Blake's heart beat out of rhythm for a split second. Then she opened his reply...

*My office. Seven o'clock. Tomorrow night.*

## 13

> *After all, I am not so violently bent*
> *upon my own opinion*
> *as to reject any offer,*
> *proposed by wise men,*
> *which shall be found equally innocent,*
> *cheap, easy, and effectual.*
> *A Modest Proposal by Jonathan Swift*

*Saturday, December 19, 2020*

*H*udson stood just beyond the kitchen entrance, listening to Karl play Betty Crocker with Blake's assistance. Once more, the irritating *and maddening* — albeit breath-stealing —woman had him hiding and spying in his own home.

"Let's add some stabilizer, since you want the meringue nice and tall," Blake said.

"What do we use for stabilizer?" Karl asked.

"Something acidic," she replied. "Do you have cream of

tartar or plain white vinegar? Even some fresh lemon juice will work."

"We probably have all three; Anita stocks the kitchen pretty well so she has what she needs when she comes to cook for us," Karl explained.

"Anita? You have a private chef?"

Hudson shook his head; by her judgmental tone, Blake hadn't bothered hiding her true feelings one bit.

"I wouldn't say that," Karl laughed. "But we do have a housekeeper, Mrs. de la Fuente, and her daughter comes to cook for us a few days each week. She's *amazing*," Karl said. Dreamily.

Hudson frowned.

"*She's* amazing, or her cooking is amazing?" Blake asked.

"Both," Karl said with a heartfelt sigh.

Did Karl have a crush on Anita? Since when? They'd practically grown up together, could be brother and sister, for heaven's sake.

"It's like that, huh?" Blake teased the boy.

"I wish," he admitted. "But Anita only has eyes for culinary school. That's why she cooks for us: she says she needs the practice. The truth is, Hudson wanted to pay for her school, but Anita is proud. She refuses to take handouts, as she calls his offer. But it's not charity. Anita is family. Her parents have been a huge part of Twin Oaks since they got married a really long time ago; they're integral to the ranch's success."

"So Hudson tried to talk her into a job — serving him — rather than insisting she go to school?" Blake assumed, again with judgmental negativity in her tone.

"Hudson?" Karl scoffed. "No. Hudson demands school above all else. Trust me; it's all we hear about... *Study more, party less... Y'all better not skip class one more time to practice roping; you've got plenty of time for both... Your grades ARE your job...* He's like a broken record, going on and on and on."

Hudson scowled. Someone had to hold those boys responsible.

Then his expression lightened when he accepted the back-handed compliment for what it was.

*Take that, Little Miss Priss, so determined to think the worst of me. I'm not such a bad guy!*

"So, Anita *is* in school?"

"Yeah, she's a freshman in college, but we all got sent home this year because of COVID. She's a Hospitality Management major and studies culinary science at Auburn University, which is a good twelve hours from where I go to college to rodeo."

The dejection in Karl's voice prompted Hudson to sneak a peek around the wall.

Karl did indeed look like a man walking the plank. Blake wore a beautiful sympathetic smile.

"It'll all work out in due time. You just have to believe," she assured Karl. Then she bumped her shoulder against his arm in encouragement. "Here, attach this bowl to the stand mixer," she instructed, sliding the stainless steel bowl his way. "Set it to medium speed. We'll watch for it to get glossy and firm enough to hold spiky peaks. And can you check the pie crusts in the oven one more time? They should be ready at any moment. Remember, just golden brown because they'll cook a little more when we put the whole thing back in to bake."

"The toothpick is clean, and the crusts looks golden brown to me," Karl said over his shoulder, bent down to hold the oven door open for inspection.

"Great," Blake said with another genuine smile. "It's time to make the chocolate pudding in that saucepan I asked you to get. We want it to be piping hot when the meringue is ready to go on top. That way the pie won't weep."

"Pies weep?" Karl asked with sad Bambi eyes. Hudson wondered the same thing.

"They do," Blake commiserated. "If the pudding cools before we get the meringue cooked on top, moisture gets trapped between the layers. It doesn't ruin the pie, but it's not fabulous."

"So, how is making a chocolate meringue pie different from other pies? Like apple pies that have crust on top…"

*H*udson didn't stick around to hear the rest of Baking 101. Instead, he ducked out and walked back to his office as quietly as he could, shaking his head in even more irritation.

*Good grief, she has me tiptoeing around my own blasted house.*

*And* distracted from his work, which had piled up on his desk over the past week — a week he'd spent deliberating far too much on Blake Fisher.

Grumbling at his lack of focus, Hudson forced his attention to a cattle deal in the works for next spring. The contracts, planning, stock management, and calculations did the trick. An hour later, he was lost in files and paperwork when Blake knocked on the doorframe to get his attention.

"Is it safe to enter?" she asked with a saucy grin.

"That depends. Is that slice of pie for me?" He dipped his head toward the towering dessert plate in her hand, but he didn't take his eyes off Blake.

Without the kitchen apron, he was free to look his fill.

She'd tucked chocolate brown winter leggings and thick colorful hunting socks into all-weather leather hiking boots, which were fur-trimmed on the inside. The *V* at her neck revealed a long-sleeved waffle tee — the color of warm and comforting oatmeal — which she'd layered under an oversized flannel button-down, an eye-catching plaid of earthy tones that reminded Hudson of the forest he treasured. A brown leather satchel hung from a long strap over her shoulder, and she'd pulled her hair into a messy knot of riotous waves on top of her head, from which tendrils had escaped at her temples and the base of her neck. The shiny peach gloss on her lips begged to be removed with a kiss.

When his eyes traveled back up her lithe and slender frame, she'd raised one eyebrow as if to ask, *Well, are you done yet?*

"I like you casual," he said with approval and zero remorse.

"My attire might be relaxed — it is Saturday, and I just spent two hours helping Karl bake pies — but don't for a second doubt that we're here to discuss business," Blake sassed back. Her prickly retorts didn't scare Hudson one bit.

"Is that why you're trying to sweeten me up?" He rose from his chair at the desk and sauntered to where she still stood in the doorway.

"Maybe this is for me," she challenged, pulling the plate back when he reached for it. Her reaction played right into his hands because she'd inadvertently removed her defensive buffer, leaving him room to step right up, nice and close.

"Oh, I'd say this is *definitely* for me," Hudson promised, his words confident yet his voice rough. Without giving Blake time to escape, he lowered his mouth to taste her lips. Yep, sweet and peachy.

When she melted into him, Hudson wrapped one arm around her waist to steady her. But with the other hand, he smoothly took the pie plate from her outstretched hand.

"Thank you," he whispered against her lips with a grin before placing a platonic peck on her nose and walking back to his desk.

She conceded defeat with an irritated grumble. Hudson smiled wider as he picked up the fork for a bite of the chocolate pie.

"Did you even read the materials I emailed over yesterday?"

"Mmm-hmm," he answered around a mouthful of meringue.

"And do you have questions about the plans and proposals?"

"Nuh-huh," he answered around another huge bite.

"Good." Her voice rang out in surprise. "In that case, I'd like to present this offer on behalf of my clients."

Blake pulled a manila folder from her bag and laid it open on his desk, hesitating midair while he lifted his plate from the spot where she obviously intended to set the contract.

Hudson didn't look at it.

He finished the scrumptious piece of pie. He strode to a bar cart where a coffeepot stayed warm on an electric hot plate. Hudson poured a cup. He took a sip, a deep breath, and his own sweet time refilling the mug. He returned to his desk and closed the folder.

"Hudson," Blake groaned. "I need you to look through those papers." She begged his cooperation with her eyes and the tilt of her obstinate chin. "Please?" she added as a last resort.

"And I need for you to understand that under no circumstances will I sell off a portion of Twin Oaks, especially for a development of any kind. Ever," he added with finality.

"You're being unreasonable," Blake argued, visibly restraining her temper. The flare only encouraged Hudson to push the envelope further. He welcomed the opportunity to see her passions ignite. He enjoyed sparring with her more than he could've possibly imagined.

"That's my right," he replied. "It's my land. And I have no desire to see it developed."

"What's so wrong with developing something that's currently lacking? It might do you some good," Blake retorted.

"Besides, it's your *family's* land," she refuted. "Have you asked for their opinions? Have you taken a vote to determine *their* wishes?"

"Ms. Fisher," Hudson said, setting down his coffee cup and standing behind his desk. "Sharp Enterprises is not a democracy. I'm the president, CEO, and managing partner. What I say goes. Period."

"Be that as it may, Mr. Dictator, you're being ignorant and close-minded. You can't control the land around Twin Oaks. Whether it's you, your children or grandchildren, or another domineering, arrogant Sharp descendant down the line, *someone* — *someday* — is going to do *something* with the Wimberly Glass property. Maybe a fertilizer plant? Or some other factory leaking chemicals into the soil? Why are you allowing your bullheadedness to get in the way of something wonderful instead? That undeveloped land is worth more to Sharp Enterprises *with* The Christmas Collection — more valuable to you, Twin Oaks, *and* Green Hills!" As Blake had gathered steam and the volume of her rant increased, Hudson had walked around the desk to stand toe-to-toe with her. He looked deep into her eyes; they flared with anger and indignation. And it fired him up.

"Don't you mean you?" he asked calmly, masking the river of heat coursing through his veins.

Her angry glare bored into his eyes. He didn't budge. She inhaled deeply and held her breath, lips compressed into a tight line of frustration.

He refused to take the bait.

She blinked rapidly three times and released the air from her lungs. Then she dropped to the couch behind her. "Yes, and me. That land is vitally important to me," she added, her voice almost broken and so quiet Hudson barely heard her. That *didn't* fire him up.

"Blake," Hudson said, completely calm and collected. "I'm

going to say it one more time: I refuse to sell or develop anything I own. But if you'd like to become the offer, I'm willing to listen."

"Excuse me?" Blake sputtered. "Me? Part of the offer?"

"Not part of," he clarified. "You *are* the offer."

**14**

*Every houseguest brings you happiness.*
*Some when they arrive,*
*and some when they leave.*
*Author unknown*

"I don't understand." Shell-shocked, Blake uttered the words.

"Are you married?" Hudson asked, not a trace of emotion in his tone.

"I think you know the answer to that." She frowned. Did he believe her to be someone who'd let a man kiss her as he had — and take part in said kisses — if she were married?

"Engaged? Promised to someone? Dating?" he persisted.

"No," she whispered, still perched on the edge of a sofa cushion. "But—"

"Fabulous. Neither am I." Hudson paused to smile — happily — at her. Then he crouched in front of her. "Blake, I won't sell a square inch of my land, but maybe you can talk me into deeding a portion to my wife."

*O*f all the entitled, officious, ridiculous, self-righteous, arrogant, overbearing…

The thesaurus entries of negative adjectives flew through Blake's head as she drove home from Twin Oaks.

Hudson wanted to marry her! In exchange for a real estate deal! And he claimed to be serious!

"It's a good idea," he'd said.

"We both get what we want this way," he'd said.

"Give it some thought," he'd said.

Then he'd bundled Blake in her coat, walked her to her car, strapped her in the driver's seat, and commanded her to *be safe getting home.* As she'd driven away, she swore he'd called out a reminder to consider his offer so they could talk about it tomorrow.

*I might not be available to talk tomorrow. These may be my final few minutes on this earth — and he's ruined them! I might get hit by a train. A projectile might fall from the sky and land right on my car. It's been known to happen. That's right… If I run off the road and hit a tree, it'll be his fault. He's crazy. Out of his mind. Insane. And now he's driving me there, too.*

Get married? To Hudson Sharp? Just to stay in Green Hills?

She couldn't!

She wouldn't!

*Sunday, December 20, 2020*

*H*e'd probably mistaken her docile and amenable behavior when she'd followed him from his office, through the Big House, and out to her car. He'd possibly believed her to be awestruck, counting her blessings because the Imperial Ruler Lord Sharp had deigned to cast his favor on poor little Blake Fisher.

Well, Hudson Alexander Sharp — *the Fourth* — could think again.

Blake was *not* singing hallelujahs; she was flat-out mad.

Madder than a hatter.

Mad enough to spit nails.

So mad she was seeing red, bristling with rage…all the idioms!

And she'd decided she would *not* be available for discussion.

Not Sunday, not Monday, not ever.

To ensure her success at remaining unavailable, she'd shut off her cell phone and silenced the ringer on her business landline.

Not ideal for a desperate and starving real estate agent, but she'd earned a day without calls and texts.

*Monday, December 21, 2020*

*B*lake still hadn't powered up her cell phone, but she did flip the ringer back on to the office phone. Then she spent an hour staring it, willing it to ring, crossing her fingers for clients to call — really loaded ones, calling from way up north, with red velvet bags of cash, and wanting to purchase a megamansion, TODAY. Not likely four days before Christmas, in Green Hills, Oklahoma — a sweet small town devoid of ostentatious megamansions…if one didn't count Twin Oaks…and a few other massive ranches in the area — but a girl could dream.

Irritated with herself for her lack of productivity, Blake refocused on what she could control. She sent the Davenport girls an update via email, a vague message along the lines of, *I've presented the offer to Mr. Sharp and hope he'll respond favorably…*

Then Blake sent Mr. Sharp an email updating him that her clients appreciated him reviewing the offer *she'd* submitted, and saying that *they* — the Davenports — looked forward to working with him in the future. In it, she refrained from using words like *counteroffer, feedback,* and *response*; she carefully avoided writing anything personal and anything he could misconstrue as a willingness to see his face or hear his voice.

Once done, Blake went about her merry day, decorating a tree in the street-facing window of Front Porch Realty, hanging Christmas lights, and even wrapping a few giant-sized empty boxes to add holiday cheer around the rocking chairs that greeted guests when they arrived.

Climbing into bed that night, Blake congratulated herself on a successful day, an accomplished day, a day without thinking about Hudson Sharp…much.

*Tuesday, December 22, 2020*

*W*ith all her work correspondence completed before 8:10 a.m. — including yet another email to Sharp Enterprises with a whole new list of pros attached, one highlighting the positive impact selling a slice of acreage would create. And since Santa hadn't seen fit to send Blake any billionaire clients, Blake set real estate tasks aside to spend time on her latest quilt project: patching a used and tearing quilt she'd bought for five dollars at a garage sale.

At Maree's insistence, Blake had begun attending the Busy Bees Quilt Guild meetings just weeks after she arrived in Green Hills. She didn't own a sewing machine — although Miss Sadie Jones had since loaned her one to keep at the office…because according to Miss Sadie, everyone had a few free minutes here and there. Blake knew virtually nothing about quilting, but she'd been hooked from the moment she'd set eyes upon the quilts and bags the members had brought for show-and-tell.

The fabric textures, the colors, and the patterns all called out to her. Each one was unique — even when using similar or identical blocks. Some used traditional designs that Blake recognized from magazine photos and catalogs she'd seen over the years. Others used free-form or modern layouts to make bold statements. Each one was impressive, with exquisite workmanship and fun, creative stitching motifs. Blake would enjoy creating works of art like that.

During the business portion of the meeting, the number of community projects and collaborations between members amazed Blake. The president's challenge provided an opportunity for every member to contribute a block based on the theme their leader had chosen for the year. How interesting to see each one's interpretation of the intentionally loose guidance the president had given them, every block unique and all of them so pretty. The Quilts of Valor committee supervised the collection and distribution of quilts to be gifted to military service members and veterans as a thank you. The Longarm Ladies volunteered to quilt charitable projects, using their commercial-style sewing machines to stitch together the three layers of a quilt — the topper, batting, and backing — at no cost to the quilt maker. And the Quilt 2 End ALZ community took part in a block-of-the-month program to support the nonprofit's mission to connect quilters with the fight to end Alzheimer's disease.

That one had been — still was — Blake's favorite. As a teenager, Blake had volunteered at nursing homes where her mom had worked in the kitchens. Inevitably, Blake had made her way to helping in the memory-care wings or floors of the facilities. She'd sit and watch television with the residents, or read them books, or sing to them. One of her favorite patients had obviously been quite a basketball player in her day. Miss Jean didn't remember Blake's name from day to day, but she hadn't forgotten how to dribble a ball. They'd use a rubber four-square ball, and Blake would playfully dribble around Miss Jean. Oh, how she'd laugh — like the purest ring of a child's joy. Then Miss Jean would steal the ball from Blake, and her eyes would light up with wonder. Once Miss Jean had the ball, she wasn't giving it up. She'd dribble, protecting the ball with her other hand, weaving around the chairs and coffee table and other patients in the long, wide corridor where they played and exercised.

The moment Blake had heard the Quilt 2 End ALZ mission, fond memories of Miss Jean, had brought tears to her eyes. She'd been excited to join the Q2EA committee and had even signed on to organize their first Quilt 2 End ALZ event, a daylong workshop and sew-in planned for the upcoming summer.

During that first guild meeting, the Busy Bees — who were indeed very busy — wowed Blake. They were making an incredible impact. Her lack of sewing and quilting skills notwithstanding, Blake had been eager to lend a hand.

During the show-and-tell portion of the meeting, guild members had shared the stories of their projects on display. Big quilts, baby quilts, old patterns, new patterns, prints, solids, basic blocks, intricate techniques… Every quilt had a fascinating backstory. And the quilters had sewn every single one with love. Blake would enjoy putting her heart into something that way. No — she *needed* to do so.

She'd placed membership that day, and almost two years later, she'd learned a ton about sewing, quilting, fabrics, piecing techniques, batting composition, finishing options, binding, embellishments, and much more. Because she lived on a shoe-string budget, Blake slowly put together a small but treasured collection of fabric and supplies: her stash of scraps from the "You Want It, You Take It" table, where guild members unloaded their leftovers; a dozen or so stunning fat quarters, a birthday gift from Maree; a fabulous pair of fabric scissors, which had been a tremendous splurge; the vintage Singer tin she'd discovered on a cluttered thrift shop shelf, which housed pouches of needles in different sizes; a few spools of thread, handed down from Miss Sadie; and a hodgepodge of trims, rickrack, and ribbons Blake had accumulated here and there.

In consideration of her empty wallet, Blake continually kept her eyes open for ways to help with guild activities that didn't require expensive purchases, like offering to chair The Longest Day event. And because most of what she bought went toward their charitable community projects, Blake had yet to make a quilt for herself. When her eyes landed on the five-dollar find at that garage sale over the summer, she knew she'd found *her* quilt.

A crazy quilt in desperate need of repair, it included a menagerie of diverse fabrics such as cottons, batiks, velvets, corduroys, and even polyesters. And the colors and patterns! Everything from delicate chintz florals to large '80s blossoms, soothing pastels to disco-inspired brights, and traditional geometrics to wild free-flowing prints jumped from the quilt top. The quilting — done with lavish ribbons, intricate trims, and bits of inexpensive bias tape — created a carnival of aesthetics, something unlike any other quilt in the world.

The quilt was Blake...pieced and stitched together with whatever could be found to support it, loved but not necessarily easy to put together, and falling apart in places, yet determined to withstand whatever life threw its way.

That was Blake's quilt.

Since buying it, she'd painstakingly and adoringly picked the threads out of any areas she needed to repair, added new fabric scraps to fill gaps, reinforced seams, and put it all back together again. In a handful of places, she'd been able to use the sewing machine, but for the most part, her quilt had required patient and precise hand-stitching. After months and months of painstaking work, light shone at the end of the proverbial tunnel. Blake had almost finished her quilt.

A jolt of cramping tension in her neck made Blake aware that she'd once again lost track of time sewing and prompted her to get up and stretch.

She laid her WIP — work-in-progress — on the chair in which she'd been sitting and went to the kitchen to check the time and brew a cup of hot tea.

She filled the kettle, lit the burner, and chose a tall, heavy mug that could keep a lot of tea hot for a long time. She took out a tea bag and spoon, and then Blake flowed through a few standing yoga postures to work the stiffness from her back and shoulders.

Goodness, 1:47 — how had it gotten so late in the day?

*Time flies when you're having fun.*

Just as the kettle whistled, the bell jangled on the front door.

"Be right there," she called out, switching off the burner and quickly pouring hot water over the tea bag in her cup. Hopeful that Santa had finally sent a savior, Blake rounded the corner into the front parlor of the old house where she'd established her business, her smile welcoming and gracious.

It fell immediately upon seeing the person standing before her.

"Oh," she uttered. "It's you."

"I brought lunch," Hudson said, seemingly unfazed by her lack of warmth.

"I don't want lunch," she said, aware but not caring that she sounded very much like a contrary child.

"Well, I do — I'm starving," he told her. With a grin and a wink, of all things.

"Humph," she grunted as he walked past her into the kitchen whence she'd just come.

"Where's a fork?" he called out.

*Grrr.*

"Don't touch anything," she warned, pivoting on the ball of a cozy-Christmas-socked foot and following her unwanted guest.

*Well, you kinda want him.*

*Shush!*

He'd set two to-go boxes on the table and opened them to reveal juicy burgers, perfectly browned French fries, and mouthwatering scoops of potato salad. Triple T's... He didn't play fair; The Three-Toed Turtle served the best hamburger in town. And when had she last eaten? She couldn't remember, which wasn't a good sign.

The burgers really did smell good.

With an unmistakably unhappy, *loud* sigh of resignation, she plunked her mug of hot tea on the breakfast table and sat at one of the place settings he'd laid out.

"Should I put your shake in the fridge for dessert?" He didn't wait for her answer, which was wise...because juvenile or not, she still wasn't talking to him.

"There's nothing in here," Hudson pointed out once he'd opened the door to place their milkshakes — another of Earl's specialties at Triple T's — inside. "I thought you lived here, above your office?"

"I do," Blake replied, eyes glued to the food on her plate. She might have to talk to him, but she refused to look at him.

Because if she looked at him, she'd see what *could* be hers. And looking at him did funny things to her insides and disastrous things to her resolve.

"Then what do you eat?"

"That's none of your business."

Hudson chuckled.

He placed their dessert in the fridge, returned to the table, and — blissfully — didn't speak again while they ate.

"Thank you," Blake allowed, standing to gather their empty food containers.

As she headed for the bin, Hudson looped an arm around her waist like a hook, and reeled her his way, until she fell onto his leg.

Blake slapped the trash back onto the table and turned an exasperated glare his way...with a dramatic huff, for added effect.

"Have you considered my proposal?" Hudson asked with a sly grin.

*Yes. Lord, help me.*

"No," she said instead, silencing the conflicting angel and devil on her shoulders, the two that refused to stop whispering unwanted advice into her ears. "I prefer to avoid lose-lose propositions."

Blake tried to stand, to escape.

Hudson didn't let her go.

"Now you're the one being close-minded." Hudson slid her hair over one shoulder and placed a soft kiss on the side of her neck, perfectly nestled under her ear, on that softest patch of skin. Tingles skittered down her arm.

Blake's breath caught — audibly, she feared.

"We'd both win," he said, his lips still warm against her skin. "You'd get your land deal, and I'd get a babysitter for the boys."

"What?" she thundered, jumping from his lap in a fit of rage. "A babysitter? For the boys?"

"They adore you. They talk about you all the time. And they actually listen to you. It's incredible," Hudson mused.

"You've lost your mind," Blake assured him.

Ignoring Hudson, and giving the table where he sat a wide berth, Blake snatched up the trash and disposed of it, washed their forks, dried them, set them back in their drawer, and marched right out of the kitchen. She turned off the light on her way out, just to make a point: Hudson could leave.

But he didn't.

His footsteps down the small hallway — in the opposite direction of the front door — alerted her he'd gone looking around her building. Moments later, splashing water indicated he'd found the bathroom sink to wash his hands. And the creak of old wooden stairs meant he'd discovered her secret.

"There's no furniture upstairs," he pointed out. Unnecessarily. Blake knew her house lacked the comforts of home.

"No," she confirmed, flouncing onto her chair. She diligently focused on resuming her sewing, placing her crazy quilt onto her lap with a bluster.

"Where do you sleep?"

"That's none of your business," she snipped. *Again.*

Hudson must've also recognized the vicious cycle they had entered because he changed the subject.

"Did you make that quilt?"

"No."

"But you're finishing it?"

"Yes."

"Where did it come from?"

"A garage sale." Blake finally looked at the interloper. She raised an eyebrow, challenging him to say something snide — that it was secondhand, shabby, or junk.

"Really? It's a work of art. How could someone toss it out that way? I mean, someone spent a ton of time creating that."

Blake would not let their mutual perspective have any bearing on her. She wouldn't!

"That's true," she conceded, but her voice came out much softer, much more *affected*, than she'd intended.

"Want to see the quilts at Twin Oaks?"

"What?" she responded, confused. How did this man so easily turn her brain to mush?

"Take a ride with me," he challenged. "Out to the ranch, so I can show you our quilts. They date all the way back to the late 1800s, when the first Mrs. Sharp — Anna — arrived in Oklahoma, bringing with her a trunk of clothes and a quilt she'd spent years making, just for her husband and their marriage bed. We have some incredible pieces. If you enjoy quilting, I think you'd get a kick out of seeing them."

The offer tempted Blake.

She wanted to see the quilt collection.

But she did *not* want to see Hudson.

*Liar.*

*I said to shush!*

"On one condition," Blake allowed.

"Shoot."

*Wouldn't I like to.*

"No more crazy talk of marriage deals," she stated.

"Only talk of crazy quilts," he pledged with a hand over his heart and an evil gleam in his eye.

## 15

*Families stitched together
with love seldom unravel.
Author unknown*

On the drive to Twin Oaks, Hudson shared interesting historical anecdotes about the buildings downtown, the city park they passed, and the neighborhoods along the way. He explained where the city boundaries had been drawn, why they'd included Daisy Lake, and how those decisions had been argued — almost to the death — in 1907, over a hundred years ago, when Oklahoma became the forty-sixth state. He shared the city council's plans to beautify the area between the Green Hills exit off the Indian Nation Turnpike and the rock structures welcoming visitors to their community.

Blake sat quietly, grateful she didn't have to come up with conversation and determined to stick to her guns.

She would not — *could not* — marry Hudson.

True, he'd turned out to be much more than the high-handed landowner she'd built him up to be in her mind.

True, he had intrigued her since that summer they met so long ago.

True, she was even more drawn to him now.

Grudgingly, Blake conceded they made a decent team, had similar perspectives…at least about some things.

She wouldn't deny they both loved Green Hills very much.

And she did have a lot of fun hanging out with the triplets. The boys certainly benefited from her guidance…like a big sister they'd never had, but needed — someone to help them and support them as only a sister can. They hadn't been in trouble one time in the twelve days she'd known them. And that was really saying something.

If Blake was being honest, Hudson's kisses did something wonderful to her.

When they were together, the world became less of an uphill battle, like the hills and hurdles ahead transformed into adventures to tackle, rather than obstacles to overcome.

And when she was in his arms, the world shifted on its axis. Everything clicked into place when he held her. In those moments, Blake found a balance and a peace she'd never even dreamed existed.

"We're here," Hudson said, pulling Blake from her maelstrom of truths. The gentleness of his voice showed he knew she'd been miles away in thought.

She nodded with a small smile, but she didn't respond.

By the time she'd unbuckled her seat belt, gathered her purse, and slid into her coat, Hudson appeared at her door, opening it, and offering a hand to help her down from the large vehicle.

*That man is always offering something.*

When she stepped to the ground, Hudson didn't retreat, so

the space between them shrunk to near nothingness. Dropping her hand, he lifted her chin until they gazed into one another's eyes. He stroked her cheek with the back of his fingers; Hudson watched the trail of his touch.

Blake followed his focus…from her cheek, to her forehead, then to her eyes, and finally settling on her mouth. When she thought he'd lean in to kiss her — *yearned for him to kiss her* — Hudson gave a half shake of his head and with an introspective half grin said, "Let's go see those quilts."

"This is the craft barn," he announced, sliding back an enormous wooden door, traditional in style but stained or aged to a deep umber instead of painted red with white trim.

"You have a craft barn?" Blake said, gaping at the magnificent space.

"That we do," Hudson chuckled.

He flipped a series of wall switches to turn on brilliant lights, illuminating a space unlike anything Blake had ever seen.

"Hudson, this is unbelievable," she marveled.

A workroom unfolded before her. Sturdy L-shaped tables — each outfitted with electrical access, individual lights, a pressing board, a cutting mat, a trash can, and a cup holder — formed a huge *U* at one end of the space. Felt covered the walls behind the desks to create personal design space; a colorful cushion holding straight pins hung from a hook at each station. At the opening of the *U*, a rustic wooden table held a board covered in silver heat-protective fabric, providing the perfect surface for pressing, cutting, and organizing. Behind it, an enormous television — more like a theater screen — hung on a wall.

Blake ran her fingers along the desks, imagining what she could create with such room to spread out, with a room full of quilters to learn from, and with free time to explore her new hobby.

"Come on," Hudson said, grabbing her hand. "The museum is this way."

"Museum?" she repeated in wonder.

On their way to the front of the barn — apparently they'd entered through the back — they passed two longarm machines with computers attached and yet more lights overhead; a long wall of built-in shelves holding fabric bolts, folded scraps, and sewing books; a full pegboard wall of tools, rulers, scissors, hoops, templates, and threads organized on hooks. Along the third wall, a wide bookcase — painted creamy white and distressed to look at home in the barn — housed scrapbooking supplies, magazines, colorful papers, large cutters, jars of buttons and flowers and paperclips and doodads, and oodles of stickers grouped in clear acrylic boxes. Littering the floor in front of the bookcase and built-in shelves, skeins and balls of yarn, chains of abandoned crochet, and colorful knitting needles overflowed and poked out from silver buckets — the metal kind used for farm and ranch chores.

Blake's eyes couldn't take it all in; her mind couldn't process all that she saw.

Speechless, she let Hudson pull her through the crafter's heaven, down a spacious hallway, and through skillfully carved wooden doors, at least fourteen feet tall and adorned with black iron nailheads, hinges, and hardware. He opened one door and gently pushed her through.

"Ready?" Hudson asked before flipping the light switch.

Blake braced herself for another shock to the system... She should've tried harder.

*Oh, Alice... Now I understand how you felt falling down the rabbit hole. Talk about a wonderland.*

"You have a museum," she uttered, blown away by the glass display cases, the antique sewing machines, shelves of scrapbooks running floor to ceiling the entire width of the back wall. Quilts hung from hinged arms, like those carpet stores used to display rugs, so one could turn the page of Twin Oaks' history, written in the stitches of heirloom quilts. The colors, the patterns, the skill of those whose hands had created such artwork sent chills and thrills through Blake.

What did it mean to be part of a history so rich, so deep?

"This is the quilt I mentioned earlier: Anne's wedding quilt, which she worked on as a child, then a teenager, and finally a young bride, waiting for word she could travel west to join her husband, wherever he'd determined to build their life together."

"And that was in 1881, when Green Hills was established?"

"Her husband, Tobias Karl Benjamin von Sharp—"

"Yes, I remember," Blake interrupted with a smile. Against her better judgment, she warmed up to Hudson. In such a setting, it was impossible to give him the cold shoulder.

"Well, as you know" —Hudson grinned back— "he followed Captain Payne as far as the entrance to Twin Oaks — which at the time was literally two small matching oaks — in 1881. But it took him some time to gain the trust and respect of the Native Americans he wanted to befriend. He needed to buy cattle, build shelter, and establish a foundation before he sent for Anna."

"How long were they apart?"

"Almost five years."

"Five years!" Blake couldn't imagine it. "Were they in love? When they married, was it an arranged marriage or a love match? If their families arranged it, those five years must've been riddled with worry and concern about what was to come. And if it was true love, the time apart must've been torture."

"The letters they wrote to one another point to a combination of the two scenarios. Both their families had emigrated from Germany and knew one another in the community where they'd landed in America. Their parents took credit for encouraging the engagement. They were very young when they married — Tobias nineteen and Anna only sixteen years old. Their wedding took place the morning he left for Indian Territory, so they couldn't have known one another well, at least not as husband and wife. But those letters are most certainly love letters. Anna filled hers with ideas and hopes and dreams for their life together; Tobias filled his pages with descriptions of the hills, the trees, the people, and his longing for her to see it. And I know this: Anna rode the train west to Van Buren, Arkansas — which was the closest depot to Green Hills — where Tobias met her on April 2, 1885. She gave birth to my great-great-grandpa, Otto Hudson Sharp, exactly forty weeks later, on January 7, 1886. Take from that what you will, but I'd say they were pretty happy to see one another."

He gave her a knowing glance, to which Blake merely shrugged, not willing to encourage his ego with agreement, but not exactly disagreeing with him, either.

She continued perusing the Sharp family heirlooms, studying photographs and journal entries and letters displayed with folded baby quilts and handmade layettes, stylish purses and bags from every decade, hatboxes overflowing with intricately addressed envelopes and canceled stamps of all denominations, and more memorabilia than a sizable exhibit might include.

"Y'all do like to recycle names," Blake commented while skimming a letter Hudson Alexander Sharp — *the First*, Blake presumed — had written to his parents, Otto and Sarah, about a girl he'd met in Texas and wanted them to meet. Dated October 21, 1928, Hud explained he was writing to them late in the night and by candlelight because he couldn't wait even an hour to tell them of the girl he'd seen across the midway at the State Fair. She'd been standing in line for tickets to see *Desert Song*, an operetta playing in the main auditorium, but it being the final night of the fair, they'd already sold all the tickets. Bud, Hudson's best friend and travel companion—

"Hud and Bud?" Blake asked over her shoulder, casting a comical look upon Hudson — her Hudson.

*No, not your Hudson. Hudson the Fourth.*

"Hey, they say truth is stranger than fiction," Hudson grinned indulgently. "Perhaps it's funnier, too."

The letter described in great detail how, since Hud had an extra ticket, he'd offered it to the girl. Thrilled with her change of luck, she'd asked how much he'd take for it, but he hadn't wanted money.

The Sharps had plenty of that…even in 1928, it seemed.

Hud said he answered, "I'd simply like the opportunity to sit next to you while they sing."

Impressed with his smooth yet endearing answer, the girl had introduced herself as Evelyn Long and accepted his offer to join him for the show. By the time the evening ended, Hud knew Evelyn belonged to a prestigious and wealthy Dallas family. He'd also learned she intended to attend the University of Texas in Austin in the fall, hoping to study music. Hud waxed poetic about her pristine blue eyes, the bouncy curls of her dark brown hair, and the effervescent energy with which she spoke. He even asked his parents' permission to bring her to Twin Oaks over his upcoming holiday break from school.

"Did Evelyn accompany Hud home that Christmas?" Blake found herself entranced in the love story, from reading one silly letter. But it wasn't silly, not really. It was just difficult to reconcile that these historical characters and events weren't detached subjects in a random museum. They were Hudson's heritage, his history, and his story.

"Not only did he bring her home, he married her on Christmas Eve."

"Of that same year?"

"1928," Hudson confirmed without even looking at the letter she read. "This is them…" He walked to another glass case, one that reached from floor to ceiling and displayed several wedding gowns on full-size dress forms. Beside each dress, a large portrait rested in an ornately scrolled floor easel, a portrait of a bride wearing her beautiful gown and standing next to a handsome Sharp man.

Blake walked to Hudson's side to admire the dress — all the dresses — and to marvel at the couples. She was particularly taken with the women in those pictures, women who'd had the courage to accept the offers they'd received from the men at their side. How had they done it? By faith alone? Believing that undeveloped love could grow into something strong and tangible by willing it into existence? Had they made it so? Or had the love already been there, such a love that they'd had no choice but to throw caution to the wind and join the forces of this family?

"October 21 to December 24… They didn't waste any time," Blake commented, dragging her thoughts back to the couple they'd been discussing.

"When you know, you know," Hudson replied.

"Hmm," Blake responded, not sure what else she could say to his unrestrained confidence.

"They lived a wonderful life, together and devoutly in love until the day they died," Hudson said.

"They died together? In an accident?" Blake asked, her heart breaking a bit at the thought their love had been cut short.

"Yes," Hudson answered, "and no. They died the same day — New Year's Eve, 2008, but not in an accident. Hud took his final breath just minutes after Evelyn took hers, cuddled together, holding hands. He was ninety-nine, and she was ninety-seven; we'd celebrated their eightieth anniversary just a week before. Whether old age or dementia, they'd both slipped a little mentally...forgot things more often, didn't realize they'd already said this or that. But they never forgot one another. They never stopped being in love."

"Wow," Blake said in reverence. "That's quite a story."

"Our family is filled with them."

"That's a whole new level of pressure," Blake quipped.

"In what way?" Hudson's expression of consternation told Blake all she needed to know... In Hudson's world, things didn't go wrong. No one bailed when something went sour. Blake couldn't envision a life like that.

"A track record like that means the family expects you to get it right. The first time," Blake added. "There's no room for error, no space to make a mistake. Or choose the wrong person."

"I'm sure we'll make mistakes," he vowed, looking down at the toe of his boot, which rubbed a speck of invisible dirt on the stained concrete floor of the museum. He'd never let a thread of vulnerability show before — at least the grown-up Hudson hadn't. That tiny shred of humility filled her eyes and her chest with tingling warmth. His openness made it hard to breathe. This strong, unyielding man wore responsibility like a cowboy's vest, one made of the supplest, softest leather, one molded to fit. Did his willingness to let her see a weakness mean he'd let his wife help carry the burden? Would he let her share the load as a partner, not another Sharp Enterprises possession?

"We all do," Blake reassured him.

Chin close to his chest, only Hudson's eyes lifted to meet hers. "But we'll work through them, together."

"I'm sure you will," Blake agreed, making sure they were talking about the hypothetical *we*, not the Hudson-and-Blake *we*. She needed to re-establish her boundaries with Hudson — for herself. Because they'd become horribly muddled. "Thanks for the VIP tour. Your family — your history — is quite incredible."

"We're an open book — many books and diaries and journals, actually. I'm happy to share more anytime you're interested."

*Oh, I'm interested.*

*Shush!*

"It's getting late, and the sun's going down awful early these days; I better head home. Do you mind driving me?"

"Can I talk you into staying for dinner?"

*Yes.*

"No. Thank you," she tacked on, trying to keep the peace and preserve the truce they seemed to have found.

They walked back through the dream-come-true crafting workshop, closed up the barn, and drove to town. The drive flew by; too much weighed on Blake's mind to make small talk. Hudson didn't say much either, so perhaps he felt the same.

He pulled his truck next to the curb in front of Front Porch Realty and put it into park.

"Hudson?" Blake asked. His hand was poised on the handle to come around and help her from the truck. Always a cowboy, such a gentleman...despite his tendency to take charge and his expectation to be in control.

He looked across the cab of the truck to see what she wanted.

"Did you read the additional materials I emailed you yesterday?"

"Of course," he said, as if she were crazy for thinking he wouldn't.

"And what do you think?" With the other documents, she'd sent updated projections for The Christmas Collection; every financial forecast the Davenports had purchased showed the same thing: the holiday shop and complementing elements would be a tremendous success.

"That I'm ready to negotiate whenever you are. You know my terms, Blake… The ball's in your court."

With that, Hudson walked her to the door, the heat of his hand at the small of her back burning through the heavy coat between his palm and her flesh.

Blake unlocked the door, and Hudson opened it. But he didn't act as though he wanted to go in, and she didn't invite him to do so.

She did, however, take a moment to look deep into his eyes, trying to decipher his intentions, to figure out his endgame. Hudson let Blake look her fill.

She hoped he'd kiss her goodbye.

He didn't.

Instead, he tipped his cowboy hat, walked down the porch steps, climbed into his big white truck, and drove away.

When he left, the questions cluttering Blake's mind remained: Should she get married? To Hudson Sharp? Just to stay in Green Hills?

She wouldn't!

She couldn't!

*Right?*

## 16

*You can't beat a good donut.*
*Paul Hollywood*

$\mathcal{H}$udson didn't hear from Blake on Wednesday.

He suspected she was taking time to sort through what he'd shared, important things she needed to know before saying *yes*.

For one, she'd be marrying the whole Sharp family, not just him. They'd love her, protect her, and be there for her — always — just as he would. She'd mentioned her mother several times, and Hudson suspected they had a close relationship. He'd also concluded that as the only child of a single mom struggling to make ends meet, Blake had lived a somewhat solitary life...and that life had forced her to do for herself from a rather young age. Hudson needed her to know she could count on him, on *them:* the entire Sharp clan.

She'd also be committing for the long haul. Sharps married only once, so once had to be enough. His parents had raised Hudson to believe that when the going got rough — and he wasn't naive enough to think they wouldn't have tough times

— Sharps doubled down, dug in deeper, and found a way through. Together, forever.

And forever would take place on the Twin Oaks ranch. Of course, she wanted that: a way to stay in Green Hills, a way to save her business and secure her future in their quaint small town. She might see that aspect of their deal as to her advantage, but in reality, it was his ace in the hole. Whether or not she realized it, Hudson and Green Hills were a packaged deal. Spending years seeing her in town, possibly married to someone else — carrying someone else's children — spelled out a torture Hudson could not handle. No, if she got Green Hills, she'd have to take Hudson with it… As the saying went, one had to take the good with the bad.

Hudson grinned. He was pretty sure she'd decided he wasn't all *that* bad. She didn't hate his kisses, judging by her fiery response and participation. She hadn't minded relaxing against him, snuggling in his arms when they rode Justice; no, she fit just right. And when she let her feisty walls down, she seemed to downright enjoy spending time with Hudson. Indeed, he was quite sure about it: she liked him.

His grin turned to a chuckle.

Sharing those few stories about his family, showing her a brief chapter of their history, had been a calculated move. He'd done it to give her something to think about.

But how long was he willing to let her ponder?

*Thursday, December 24, 2020*

Thirty-six hours. That turned out to be the magic number.

Christmas Eve festivities began at the crack of dawn in Green Hills, so Hudson strode onto Blake's front porch and knocked on the door at precisely 5:53 a.m., piping hot coffee and a box of donuts in hand.

She answered the door in layers... The too-long sleeves and too-long pant legs of long johns stuck out from beneath the cuffs of thick flannel button-down pajamas. Over that she wore an oversized holey sweatshirt that had seen much better days. On top of that she had thrown on a calf-length bathrobe made of tacky velour. A crocheted scarf encircled her neck, and the same ivory beanie she'd worn to ride horses sat atop her head, smooshing a rebellious tangle of cascading auburn waves. She'd even added a pair of emerald green mittens, the kind kids wore to build snowmen or to save their fingers in a snowball fight.

"Why are you here?" she asked in the sexiest grumpy-in-the-morning voice he'd ever heard, raw with sleep, very vintage Katharine Hepburn. Just hearing it made getting up early enough to have his ranch chores finished by 5:00 a.m. well worth the lack of sleep.

"Why are you still in bed? On Christmas Eve? Dressed like that?" Hudson loved answering questions with questions... It really kept his opponent on her toes.

Except she wasn't having it. Without another word, Blake closed the front door solidly in his face. His certainty that she was joking took a nosedive — along with his stomach — when the deadbolt clicked into place.

"Blake? Come back and open this door," he called.

No response.

"I'm not leaving until you do," he threatened.

Still nothing.

"I'm willing to camp out on your front porch all day — all Christmas," he declared.

Crickets — hypothetically, seeing how crickets chirp during the hot summers, and it was actually the end of December, and the day's forecast said snowy with a high of thirty-seven degrees.

"Should I bang on this little decorative window first? I'm thinking it's the least expensive for you to replace."

"That's breaking and entering," she said from the other side. Ah, she hadn't gone too far.

"I'm friends with Chief Crockett...and every other police officer in Green Hills. Worst I'll get is disturbing the peace. That's just a misdemeanor," Hudson replied.

"Why am I not surprised?" she grumbled, along with something about *ridiculous, small-town, rich,* and *entitled*... He couldn't hear her protestations clearly through the heavy door. Probably just as well.

"And it would only be breaking; I can't fit through that window, so I'd have to beat down the big picture window here by your porch swing." He knocked on the window in question, just hard enough to make it shake in the frame.

"You wouldn't dare," Blake bellowed. Her voice — still sexy as all get-out — sounded more awake. Progress.

"It's cold out here," Hudson pointed out, changing tactics.

"Good."

"Your coffee won't stay hot for long."

"That's okay — I don't drink coffee," she assured him. Yes, awake, yet still on the other side of a locked door.

"These poor donuts are turning into frozen hockey pucks."

Pause.

Feet shuffling on hardwood floors.

Deadbolt unlatching.

Door opening.

Hudson's heart grew three sizes at the sight of Blake — hands on hips, frown on lips — glaring up at him with daggers sharp enough to do real damage.

"Good morning," he greeted her, sealing the moment into his memory. He never wanted to forget how it felt, the second he knew he wouldn't have to live without her. Whatever it took, he'd make Blake his.

"I'll take the donuts." She reached out a hand, palm up.

"They come with strings attached."

"What strings?"

"Me," he answered. "And a day full of Christmas Eve, Green Hills style."

She'd lived in town the previous Christmas, but she couldn't have been at the festivities last year. Hudson would've remembered seeing her there. Of that, he was sure.

"Fine. Come in," she groused, ever so graciously.

*And she says I'm a grinch,* he thought with a chuckle.

"You're in for a treat," Hudson promised, looking forward to the day. Come to think of it, he hadn't been so excited to spend a Christmas Eve off the ranch since he was a little boy.

"Why does the treat have to begin so early?" she complained, filling a teakettle with water from the kitchen sink.

"Because it's over by lunchtime, so families can settle and have dinner before candlelight services at the churches around town," Hudson explained.

"I've heard about this crazy Green Hills tradition, but I spent Christmas with Mama last year and missed seeing it in person." Blake busied herself setting the kettle on the cooktop and lighting the burner — the old-fashioned way with a match. She took two mugs from the cabinet, poured Hudson's styrofoam cup of coffee in one, and placed it in the microwave to reheat.

"Well, you're in luck this year… I know all the best places to get all the best treats." He waggled his eyebrows to make his point. Looking over her shoulder at Hudson, she laughed, shaking her head at his antics. Hudson could've sworn he'd just received his first gift for Christmas.

While she bustled around the kitchen, selecting a red tin of tea bags from the pantry, taking two small Christmas plates from a holiday display on the kitchen counter, and grabbing green, gold, and white plaid napkins from a drawer in a hutch, Hudson sat at the small table where they'd eaten lunch two days earlier. He studied the sparse yet intentional decorations. If minimalism could also be homey, Blake had mastered it, and in a way that reflected both her personality and her talent at staging spaces. The only thing he couldn't figure out was the temperature, which was not warm and inviting.

"Why's it so cold in here?" Hudson asked when Blake set their hot drinks next to the donut box and joined him at the table.

"Oh, the heater's acting up again…happens all the time. Mr. Mira ordered the part yesterday."

"Did George say when he'd have it to install? It's really frigid in here, and the weather is only supposed to get worse over the next couple of days."

"He put a rush on it, but with the holidays, he said it won't arrive until next week. He'll get to me as soon as it gets here. We have a very good — very ongoing — relationship. He and Mrs. Mira have been quite kind to me."

"Blake, you can't stay here until then."

"I have nowhere else to go," she mumbled around a healthy bite of a vanilla-filled chocolate eclair. "Mama's working a holiday house party in Atlanta that starts today and doesn't end until New Year's Day. That's why I stayed in Green Hills for Christmas."

"You have Twin Oaks."

"I do *not* have Twin Oaks. You have Twin Oaks. And Christmas with your family."

"You *could* have Twin Oaks," he pointed out, watching closely for her reaction and trying to convince himself he didn't care what it revealed.

She didn't reply, but her cheeks flushed a bit. He took that as a good sign. Of course, frostbite could also be the cause of it.

"Besides, it's just me and the boys. My grandparents house-hop year-round to visit family, my aunt and uncle are midway through a string of business meetings and celebrating Christmas wherever they happen to be this week, and Mom and Dad are too busy sailing their way around the world to make it home this Christmas. It's the darnedest thing," he added, more to himself than to Blake. His grandparents, aunt, and uncle he could understand, but what in the world had gotten into his parents? They'd eschewed all their responsibilities and dumped everything on their children, specifically Hudson!

"I can't stay at the ranch," Blake said, refocusing his wandering mind.

"You *can*," he countered, reminding her that all she had to do was say *yes*.

*If only she would let it be that simple.*

"At least pack a bag. If the weather takes the predicted turn for the worse, you'll have an option. Please?" he tacked on when she hadn't agreed quickly enough for his liking.

"Oh, all right," she relented. "I'm going to run through a hot shower and get dressed and—"

"Pack a bag," he filled in for her.

"And pack a bag," she repeated, finally giving up on her determination to tough it out in the freezing house. "Give me thirty minutes, and I'll be ready to go."

"Perfect," he said, truly joyful. "I'll be waiting in my truck…where it's warm."

## 17

*So Joseph also went up from the town of*
*Nazareth in Galilee to Judea,*
*to Bethlehem the town of David,*
*because he belonged to the house and line of David.*
*He went there to register with Mary,*
*who was pledged to be married to him*
*and was expecting a child.*
*While they were there,*
*the time came for the baby to be born,*
*and she gave birth to her firstborn, a son.*
*She wrapped him in cloths and placed him*
*in a manger, because there was*
*no guest room available for them.*

*And there were shepherds living out in the fields*
*nearby, keeping watch over their flocks at night.*
*An angel of the Lord appeared to them,*
*and the glory of the Lord shone around them,*
*and they were terrified.*
*But the angel said to them,*

> *"Do not be afraid. I bring you good news that will*
> *cause great joy for all the people.*
> *Today in the town of David*
> *a Savior has been born to you;*
> *he is the Messiah, the Lord."*

### Luke 2:4–11

*I*f Blake had learned anything since moving to Green Hills, it was that Green Hills knew how to do community!

The residents and business owners had that fact on full display for Christmas Eve. Shops around the downtown square — decorated to the nines, with painted and dressed windows, elegant displays, and a forest's worth of garland and boughs — opened by 7 a.m., providing time to shop, for those who'd waited to find goodies for their loved ones and those who needed one more gift. The grounds around the courthouse buzzed with people and activities: Santa heard Christmas lists and posed for photos with children, and a few yards away, Mr. Mitchell, one of the local pastors, and teens from his church took turns reading the Christmas story from Luke 2 beside a live nativity scene; on another side of the square, carolers sang traditional holiday songs and beloved Christmas hymns; and food was everywhere: a coffee truck, a hot chocolate station, an apple booth with spiced wassail and apple turnovers and apple bread and apple cake, a mobile taco cart Earl had constructed to bicycle Triple T's famous breakfast tacos around the grounds, and a full tent of donuts — just to name a few.

"How do people eat all this, and then go home to fix a big Christmas dinner?" Blake marveled.

"It's all about pace and resting," Hudson told her with an expression of mock wisdom. "And a few games of football in the yard between meals. Those always help."

"I'm sure those are calm and friendly at your house," she teased.

"Well," Hudson drawled, "they're *something*, that's for sure." The cringing look of apology, hours in advance, explained all Blake needed to know.

"I bet the boys add a whole new meaning to the phrase *holiday enthusiasm*," she said with a laugh. "I'd like to get them a little something while we're looking around."

"You don't need to do that," Hudson said. "You being there is all the gift we need."

It was sweet of Hudson to say, and certainly there wasn't anything Blake could get the Sharp men that they couldn't get for themselves. But having small gifts to share, a token of thanks for each of them — for including her in their celebration, but more for their friendship — on Christmas morning meant a lot to Blake.

"I want to," she replied. "I'll meet you back here at Maree's shop in an hour…so I can browse without you for a bit."

"Nothing for me," he instructed, eyes twinkling above his ever-present almost-but-not-quite-there smile, introspective and sage, not grumpy and hateful as Blake had assumed when they'd first met.

Still waters run deep.

She shrugged while pivoting away, neither agreeing nor arguing, but knowing in her mind exactly what she hoped to find for him.

"Make it *two* hours," she hollered at him over her shoulder, not waiting to ensure he heard.

Blake had a blast browsing through the shops and the booths. She greeted familiar faces and gave holiday hugs to those she knew from town. She missed seeing the Davenports but imagined they were having a wonderful time together in

Kansas City, spoiling Janie Lyn and Max's new baby boy around the clock.

While she strolled, Blake sipped on a cup of warm cider — tangy with apples and oranges, sweet with pineapple and honey, and spicy with cinnamon and clove. After the size of the donut she'd had for breakfast, she couldn't even think of snacking, but several items caught her fancy.

In the end, she purchased a tin of candied pecans and a peach pound cake to share with Hudson and the boys. Then, she shopped...

Filed in the back of an old wooden crate, covered in dust at the back of the resale shop, Blake found Alabama's *Christmas* album for Tobi; she selected one other record to go with it, hoping he had a turntable. In a booth the Green Hills Library had set up on the courthouse steps, Blake discovered a fabulous, barely used copy of Mary Berry's *Desserts and Confections* for Karl. And in the antique store, an inexpensive vintage oil painting of a horse standing proud in a green field caught Blake's eye; the frame had seen better days, but despite its age and chipped edges, the ornate and interesting frame possessed a unique beauty Bennie would appreciate.

Hudson proved more difficult to shop for... *Imagine that: Hudson being difficult.*

Luckily, she found the perfect thing!

The hours flew by — successfully, but quickly. Packages in hand, Blake arrived at Maree's shop, Main Street Design, at the same moment Hudson stepped from Mrs. Dawsey's, the candy store a few doors down.

"Mission accomplished, I see," Hudson called out as he walked toward her.

"It's a good thing I was on a tight schedule," Blake confessed. "I could've easily gone overboard out here. I can see why Janie Lyn and the girls are so excited to stock Christmas goods from local artisans year-round — such talent!"

"So, you're ready to sign on the dotted line?" Hudson stopped walking, but not until he'd invaded her personal space. They were face to face. His was equal measures hopeful and teasing. Blake could tell hers was flushed. Looking into Hudson's eyes, especially when he allowed her to see his playful side, did that to her. Standing so close she could feel his heat and smell his cologne — forever mixed with virility and the scent of being outdoors — made her nerves skitter and her skin blush. Not to mention what he did to her pulse.

He'd affected her the same way when she was a teenager; why should it be any different as an adult?

But was that enough to saddle him to a wife he didn't love?

*And, of course, I don't love him.*

*But I could.*

*I might.*

With so many thoughts — conflicting and confusing — running amuck in her mind, Blake forgot to answer.

Luckily, Hudson let her off the hook when, with an indulgent smile, he chucked her under the chin and reached for her bags. "Can I put these in the car for you? That way you can keep looking," he offered.

*Does he mean looking at the holiday booths, or at him?*

*Can I do both?*

*Snap out of it!*

The internal reprimand worked, and Blake strung coherent words together. "That's okay. I'm finished...for now," she added, just in case they were, indeed, talking about how she couldn't seem to take her eyes off Hudson.

What had come over her?

One minute she'd been holding on to her anger, affronted that Hudson wouldn't take her seriously as a real estate agent, wouldn't be reasonable about the contract she'd presented on behalf of her clients. The next minute, she was arguing with herself over that stupid counteroffer he'd made.

*Either like him or don't.*

*Stay or go.*

*Let the business thrive or fail.*

*Be Blake Fisher or Mrs. Hudson Sharp.*

*Just pick already.*

*You can't have it both ways!*

*Or can I?*

"Where to next?" Hudson asked, again pulling her from a blistering mental monologue.

"Nowhere for me," she answered. "I have everything I need, if you're still insistent I join your family for Christmas Eve."

Blake looked away as soon as she'd said the words. She didn't want to see the emotions pass through his eyes, nor the way his sexy smile softened his lips.

Watching the world flash by her window, Blake didn't speak again on the drive to Twin Oaks.

She continued to question, second-guess, berate, and excuse her wayward thoughts, her irrational hopes, and her silly dreams. Why did she want it all?

But why couldn't she have it all?

Why couldn't a girl have the self-designed, highly successful career *and* the strong, commanding cowboy who makes her heart flutter by merely existing?

*Because that's a fairy tale.*

*Because I live in the nearly empty real estate office that has no heat... Because I drive a fourteen-year-old SUV that needs new paint and likes to leak oil... Because my family tree contains one branch, a sweet mother who's struggling even harder than I am to make it through another day.*

*Because I don't belong in a place like this,* Blake reminded herself as Hudson clicked a garage door opener for the entry gates at the ranch — the same gates she'd had to case and sneak through to gain access to the hallowed grounds.

Blake tilted her head to look up at the towering trees she'd studied that day. The gargoyle branches still seemed to laugh at her, flaunting the fact she was miserably out of place.

"Welcome to Christmas at Twin Oaks," Hudson said, his tone welcoming, but also proud. He genuinely seemed glad to have Blake at the ranch.

He'd let her brew and stew on the drive, hadn't tried to drag her attention away from the green hills, the landscape, and the scenery they'd passed. Instead, Hudson had hummed along with Christmas songs on the radio, a veritable song in his heart.

Blake looked over at him, studying Hudson with a critical eye.

Not critical of his features — those were as masculinely gorgeous as ever — but at his intent.

Why had he been so amenable all morning?

Weren't men supposed to hate shopping and bemoan holiday tunes?

Hudson was being too nice.

Blake squinted at him in consternation. He was up to something.

Hudson only smiled in return.

"We're home," he announced after pulling the alarmingly large truck into a massive immaculate garage. "I'll grab your duffle if you get your gift bags," Hudson added, cutting the engine and opening his door.

*His home*, Blake reminded herself. *And you better not forget it.*

## 18

> *Christmas is the day*
> *that holds all time together.*
> *Alexander Smith*

*Christmas Day, Friday, December 25, 2020*

$\mathcal{W}$alking through the woods of Twin Oaks, blind to the blanket of snow beneath her feet, unaware of the animals skittering along the evergreen trees, and oblivious to the crisp breeze slicing through the brilliant sun, Blake's mind reeled.

She'd had such fun celebrating the day before.

She maintained her belief that Hudson had something up his sleeve, but she'd put that distraction aside to focus on the fellowship and festivities the boys had devised to create a special Christmas Eve...

*T*ogether, they'd laid out a deli buffet to rival the fanciest of charcuterie boards, the triplets claiming they needed full-sized sandwiches instead of bits of meat and cheese and tiny crackers. She'd laughed at their descriptions — until she saw they hadn't been kidding. They ate enough to feed an army. All four of the Sharp men were long, lean cowboys, so where did it all go?

After their huge lunch, they'd taught Blake how to play Forty-Two, and she'd discovered she did not like to lose, particularly to Hudson, even at dominoes. The triplets liked to boast and talk smack to their opponents, but true to form, Hudson sat back, silently assessing and letting his acumen speak on his behalf. He rarely lost.

Late in the afternoon, snow flurries had begun. While the triplets went out to the barn to check on and feed the horses, Hudson had built a roaring fire in the family room.

"I love a white Christmas," Blake mused, watching the flakes swirl in the breeze.

"Probably not too many of those in Alabama," Hudson commented, hunched before the fire, arranging logs as the flames grew.

"No, winters are pretty mild there. But that year I was in Oklahoma City for Christmas, we had a big dose of snow. Ice, actually — it was a messy holiday across the board. Roads were closed, heating and electricity were in and out, and my job fell apart. Not the best of times, but still a beautiful Christmas morning, covered in snow."

"If you're ever in Vegas, avoid the poker rooms," Hudson teased, but not unkindly. Rather, his tone conveyed an underlying respect.

"And why is that?" Blake asked, although she knew good and well what he meant. She had a horrible poker face;

everyone in the room always knew exactly what she was thinking and feeling. It was why she'd kept her eyes on the terrain outside the truck on their drive to Twin Oaks. It was why Hudson seemed to know exactly what dominoes she'd drawn every hand. And it was why she'd started avoiding his gaze.

Blake had gone and done the most foolish, foolhardy, fool-in-love thing she could've ever done.

She'd fallen for him. She loved — *was in love with* — Hudson Alexander Sharp, the Fourth.

She'd thought she disliked everything about Hudson: his wealth, his family, his power, his confidence, his strength, his history, his easy good looks, and even his place in the world.

But he'd turned out to be so much more. And Blake loved all of it, every facet of his character and every trait that made him the Hudson she'd gotten to know.

Love had hit her hard…like a ton of bricks. And she'd never be the same.

Finished tending the fire, Hudson rose and walked to where Blake stood at the window. Gently gripping her elbow, he turned her to face him.

"Because you're too honest," he told her, referring to the wisdom of Blake not playing games. "Even your beauty can't hide your truths."

They searched one another's eyes, looking for words and feelings neither seemed willing to voice.

Hudson lifted a hand to cup her cheek. His other hand mirrored the movement. Shifting his gaze from her eyes to her lips, Hudson framed her face with his powerful hands and lowered his mouth to hers. Blake's heart hummed. Or perhaps that was her vocal chords. Either way, she melted into his kiss, into the wall of his chest.

Her arms wrapped around his waist. She had to hold on to keep from swaying.

A low growl rumbled from Hudson. He dropped one hand and slid that arm around her back to pull her even closer.

Blake sensed Hudson straining to contain a raging need to devour, a fight she understood. Perfectly.

Fire consumed them; she felt feverish, everywhere.

Blake couldn't breathe, but she didn't need to. All she needed was Hudson.

And that thought scared her like nothing else. Enough to resurface, to stop the insanity.

"Hudson—"

His lips burned against the skin along her neck.

"Hud—"

He silenced her with another kiss.

But when he lifted his lips from hers, they didn't return to ravish her again.

His hand cradled her head, holding her forehead to his, while they both battled to catch their breath.

"I swear you've cast a spell over me," he whispered, his words teetering between praise and pain. "I—"

Footsteps in the hallway and voices chirping — loudly — interrupted whatever else he'd planned to confess.

"Oh no," Hudson groaned. He lifted his head to meet her gaze. "*I'm so sorry,*" he mouthed with a look of agony, seconds before he placed one last long pause of a kiss on her lips.

He tucked her under his arm, sidled her close to his side. Right then, a whirlwind blew through the entrance to the family room.

"Hudson Alexander! You've been holding out on us," the stunning woman declared — loudly. "Oh, wow! Juni! Alex! They're in the family room! Get in here! Just look at her!" She dropped the bags of gift-wrapped boxes she'd been carrying, along with her purse and her sunglasses, on a couch. She advanced on Blake, who'd tried dissolving into the curtains at her back, and Hudson, who'd tightened his grip on Blake so she couldn't run. Hands on hips, the woman openly surveyed Blake from head to toe. Then she brought both hands to her cheeks and declared, "My baby boys weren't exaggerating — you are gorgeous!"

She spoke in exclamation points. Every sentence declared in spirited delight. Her sparkling blue eyes matched the gleam in her voice, and could only be outshined by the blinding hunk of rock on her left ring finger. Was that a diamond or an ice sculpture?

"Trixie, really?" A man — a glimpse of Hudson thirty years in the future — grumbled under the load of luggage and coats and bags. "You left a trail of clutter and presents with every step. Oh, hello, Son," he said, casting a commiserating smile upon Hudson and Blake.

"Merry Christmas," Hudson replied, sounding both happy to see them and simultaneously heartbroken — utterly despondent. "Blake, meet my parents, Alex and Beatrix Sharp. Mom, Dad... This is Blake Fisher."

"The vulture out to take my land?" a sharp voice quipped from the doorway.

"And *this*," Hudson announced, "is my Loony Aunt Juni." Adoration overwhelmed his voice.

Not overwhelmed with suitcases, not juggling holiday gifts, and not inclined to accept the woman under her nephew's arm, Juniper Sharp sashayed over, looking like she truly belonged on a fashion runway with her long stride, elegant ivory pantsuit, and luxurious deep green velvet high heels. What a sight to behold. The woman knew her place; she knew her power. The guard trees at the entry gate stood sentry *for* Juniper Sharp. She belonged.

*Wow!*

Blake remained silent, not intimidated, but surely impressed. Back firm, shoulders back, Blake didn't shrink or back down as the three newcomers took her measure.

"You'll do," Juniper said— Agreed? Allowed? Blake couldn't be sure. But it seemed an affirmative proclamation, since the woman followed the statement with a wink at Hudson. Then she turned and left the room. "Porter and I will be back for dinner," she announced on her way out.

*P*orter turned out to be her husband, Hudson's uncle, who'd remained in the barn to saddle two horses for his wife and himself to enjoy a ride before the sun went down. Opposite his reserved and guarded wife, Porter Jamison displayed warmth, a welcome openness, and a quick smile for all.

He also turned out to be an amazing chef.

For their Christmas Eve dinner, Porter boiled pasta he'd made from scratch and frozen a few weeks earlier. He topped the pasta with a fresh and creamy homemade sauce he created using vegetables straight out of Twin Oaks' winter garden: butternut squash, leeks, onions, garlic, half-and-half, Parmesan cheese, and a secret selection of spices Porter refused to divulge. Hudson grilled chicken to serve with the pasta — a hidden talent Blake had not known about. And Beatrix — who insisted Blake call her Trixie — sautéed collard greens and baked corn on the cob, which she put in foil packets with salt, butter, and honey. All Blake contributed was guiding the triplets in mixing up a huge batch of corn bread and setting the dining room table.

The dinner — sitting at the table, with such a large family gathered around, and *actually* eating — was nothing like Blake had imagined. If a month ago, someone had asked her to describe what she thought a meal at Twin Oaks looked like, she'd have painted a picture of stuffy, stuck-up rich people in their "dressed for dinner" finery, being waited upon by a butler and understaff, too pompous to chat about their day, too lofty to share in one another's lives.

She'd have been wrong — dead wrong.

Somehow, after Blake and the boys had set the table, someone had snuck through the dining room to play Santa. When they'd carried the serving platters and vegetable bowls to the table, they found a large square box, wrapped in plaid holiday paper and tied with an exquisite ribbon, sitting on each chair. Blake held back, not wanting to intrude on their family tradition.

"I believe this is your chair," Hudson said, getting her attention simply by speaking to her. In his element, on his ranch, surrounded by his loved ones, he'd relaxed a little. His heated, smooth voice — always hypnotic to Blake's psyche — took seductive to a whole new level of heat. He pulled out the chair to the right of his, which sat at one end of the table and opposite his dad.

Blake looked at him questioningly. How could she have one? Blake hadn't even known she'd be at Twin Oaks for Christmas Eve until Hudson had demanded it over breakfast.

But right there on the tag, her name appeared in looping, elegant script.

"For me?" Gratitude and emotion threatened to overwhelm her.

Hudson must've seen the moisture in her eyes, noticed the thickening of her voice. Of course he had — Hudson missed very little.

"I'd open it before you get too excited," he warned cryptically.

She wrinkled her brow, thoroughly intrigued. Hudson shrugged, holding the gift while she sat in her chair. He handed it to her and slid into his chair. Then, as if she weighed nothing at all, he pulled her chair closer to his. Of course, Trixie saw and ahhed over the gesture. If only she knew the blackmail her son was up to, the unacceptable and indecent proposal of marriage he'd offered... Then she wouldn't welcome the newcomer so much.

Gulping down that troublesome thought on a pledge to confront it later — as if Blake thought of much else, *ever* — Blake sipped her wine and waited to follow someone else's lead.

She didn't have to wait long. Like bulls in a china shop, the triplets wasted no time ripping into their early Christmas gifts.

"What?" Tobi exclaimed with glee, shuffling through tissue paper to find the contents.

"These are awesome!" Karl added, shining a huge smile at everyone around the table.

"Mine has hippopotamuses saddled like horses," Bennie announced, like a kid...at Christmas.

All three stood by their chairs and shook out their gifts: adult long johns, each printed with a unique pattern.

"We got onesies!" Bennie added gleefully.

"Mine has gingerbread cowboys," Karl boasted.

"And mine has guitars," Tobi said, showing off the pajamas.

"Let's see yours, Hud," Alex said, a twinkle in his eye.

Blake held her breath as Hudson opened his present... slowly...building anticipation, exactly opposite of the triplets' style.

He chuckled, the sound reverberating from deep in his chest when he peered into the box.

"Nice," he said with a laugh as he pulled his union suit from the box. Bold deep green pine trees covered the fabric from collar to cuffs.

*Oh dear. I hope mine isn't printed with a woman digging for gold. Since they know about our war over the trees, that's probably precisely how they see me.*

Blake exhaled; she'd worried for naught. Delicate bundles

of mistletoe scattered across the übersoft ivory fabric of her winter pajamas.

"They're lovely," she whispered, again awed to be included.

"And send quite a message," Hudson insinuated, whispering in her ear. Shivers covered Blake from head to toe.

Luckily, the rest of the evening turned out to be less of an assault on Blake's senses.

Trixie and Alex showed off their matching red long johns; Juni and Porter had matching pajamas in green.

Before they dug into dinner, they took a five-minute break for everyone to go change into their new Christmas gear.

"You're this way," Hudson said, guiding her to the back stairs beyond the kitchen. Someone, presumably Hudson, had set her duffle bag on a gigantic bed in the middle of a beautiful guest suite. Again the extreme opposite of wealthy opulence, the heavy wooden headboard and footboard looked like someone had recently chopped it from the forest and hand sanded the logs until they glowed with welcoming warmth. The flannel sheets and thick blankets appeared soft and inviting. And an absolutely magnificent quilt, obviously hand appliquéd with holly berries and winter florals in rich, textured wool, draped across the end of the bed. A fire popped in a small cozy fireplace, heating the room and adding romantic lighting to the intimate space.

"It's idyllic," Blake told Hudson. "So homey and cute — a beautiful winter wonderland. Thank you." She blinked to clear the moisture filling her eyes. "Thank you for giving me this Christmas." Then she ducked into the bathroom to change into her union suit.

Hudson must've dashed to do the same, because when Blake emerged from the bathroom, new pajamas on with a flannel button-down over the onesie and the tails tied at her waist, big cabin socks tucked into furry boots, and her hair piled into a messy bun, Hudson stood in her doorway, leaning against the frame. He could've been any generation of Hudson Alexander Sharp, standing in his long johns and boots, a cowboy hat tilted down on his head, and a finger-tingling five-o'clock shadow itching to be touched. Hudson was a sight to behold — one that took her breath away. He had that effect on her worse and worse the more time they spent together.

Hudson lifted his head, eyes scanning Blake from the tip of her chestnut suede boots to the topknot of her haphazard hairdo. His gaze left a thrilling trail of smoldering chills.

"You're lucky we're on a five-minute clock," Hudson cautioned, backing her against the wall. "Otherwise, I'd take this sweet new side of you to heart. I thought your buttoned-up power suits did a number on me; they don't hold a candle to you like this."

Blake's head swarmed with fuzzy yearnings. Glued in place, she merely gazed into his darkened eyes.

Simultaneously, Hudson's lips touched Blake's and three voices yelled up the back stairs in unison, "Hurry up! We're starving."

"Like I said," Hudson pledged, without lifting his mouth from hers. "Lucky."

*B*lake's blood had hummed the rest of the evening... through dinner, through carols in the music room, and through Alex reading the Christmas story from the Bible in the family room before watching a holiday movie with popcorn and hot chocolate.

It had continued to hum when Hudson walked her up the stairs to say good night, and when he caressed her cheek, and when he whispered, "I'll see you in the morning."

It still hummed as Blake wandered the woods, staying out

of the house so the Sharps could enjoy their Christmas morning without an interloper.

Lost deep in thought, Blake didn't hear Justice's hooves until Hudson had ridden into the grove where she paced.

"I want to show you something," he said in lieu of *good morning* or *Merry Christmas* or any greeting of any kind.

He hopped from the saddle, boots landing firmly on the ground, and gave Blake a boost onto the horse. Then he stepped back into the stirrup and hoisted himself onto Justice's back. Without a word, he directed Justice out of the woods, across the pasture, and to an area cordoned off with survey tape.

When they reached the barrier, Hudson loosely hitched Justice to a tree and helped Blake dismount.

"What's this?" Blake asked as Hudson pulled her by the hand under the plastic tape, which he held above their heads.

"Someone suggested I consult my family, to learn their wishes for the Christmas tree farm. So, I did."

Hudson had her attention.

"It turns out Aunt Juni's preposterous planting technique created a scattering of trees beyond the thirty acres Junior had gifted her. Those seeds turned into this, a second tree lot. And while she's too sentimental to give up any of her original acreage, she'd like for this section to be made available to The Christmas Collection."

"How much?" Blake asked.

"How much...*what?*" Hudson repeated, waiting for her to fill in the blank.

He teased her, making her ask. Blake didn't care. She could save this deal, she could save her business. And she could do it without sacrificing her dignity, without agreeing to marry a man she loved, but who didn't love her.

"How much land? How much money will it take?"

Her heart pounded.

"Blake, the land has changed. The terms have not." All sense of congenial camaraderie dissipated.

"Hudson, that's crazy," she told him, striving for one of them to remain reasonable. "Why do you want to marry me? Because you feel sorry for me? Because I'm the poor girl, struggling to make it on my own? Because I can't succeed without the high and mighty, illustrious Doctor Hudson Alexander Sharp IV stepping in to save me?"

He didn't answer, and her sound, practical approach took a back seat to a myriad of emotions, including anger, frustration, and pure unrequited love.

"I don't need a pity proposal, Hudson…an arranged marriage! Someone is out there who can love me for *me*." Blake threw the words at him, and then she turned to walk away.

Hudson let her go only as far as the length of his arm before reaching out to clasp her hand, halting her progress and twirling Blake to face him.

"*I* love you," he told her.

"What makes you think you know what love is?" she countered.

"This ranch," he stated with confidence. "I've loved it since I was old enough to crawl across it, to grab handfuls of it in my pudgy baby fists. It's timeless, yet it evolves and adapts. It's resilient and strong and beautiful, no matter what the world throws its way."

"What does that have to do with me?"

"Those are the things I love most about you, too," Hudson declared, releasing her hand to run his fingers along the side of her face. Every time he touched her in such a way, he made her feel like a puzzle he wanted to figure out, like a treasure he would always handle with care.

"I sensed it when we met that summer. I saw it when you snuck onto the ranch and into my home—"

"Just the land," she interjected. "I was invited into the house."

"True," he allowed with a slight smile. "You blew me away that day — didn't back down one inch, no matter how much I growled."

Blake couldn't think of what to say.

Hudson continued.

"And the next morning, when you wanted to race me while we rode, I fell head over heels in love with you."

A sucker punch to the solar plexus would've left more air in her lungs.

"I've never known fear like the wave of terror that flowed through me when I thought you'd collide with Bennie on the trail. I realized right then that I couldn't live without you."

Still, Blake couldn't speak. In fact, one could've knocked her down with a feather.

"This plat includes twenty-seven acres. It borders the Wimberly Glass Factory in a crescent, so instead of a small section of trees to one side of the holiday compound y'all have drawn up, The Christmas Collection will have access to a stunning backdrop, wide across the property. Sharp Enterprises would like to do a long-term lease, twenty-five or fifty years, whichever the Davenports prefer, at no charge. The only terms are that the current CEO of Sharp Enterprises have final approval of any developments or improvements added to the land and that no fee be required to access the tree portion of the business. Aunt Juni wants everyone to enjoy the tree farm for free."

"So you don't want to marry me?" Blake should've been elated about the lease agreement. It was everything she'd hoped for. But she couldn't get past the part where he'd said, *The only terms…*

The *only* terms.

Blake's lungs deflated with a sad sigh. She should've said *yes* sooner.

"Oh, I still want to marry you," Hudson assured her. "I'd say *I do* today, if you'd agree. But not for the land deal."

He reached into his pocket and pulled out a ring, an exquisite square diamond surrounded by clusters of beautiful tiny pearls and sparkling diamonds, set on a thick gold band.

Blake's stomach did a flip. Her heart raced uncontrollably.

"Marry me because you love me." Holding her hand, waiting for a sign he could slide his ring onto her finger, Hudson proposed, more eloquently the second — or was it the third — time around. He looked at her with passion and hope in his eyes.

"I do, you know — love you — whether I want to or not," Blake admitted. "I've spent my whole life hating everything I thought you represented: an easy life; the rich boy who has it all; a man who never has to lift a finger, who beckons and calls, and everyone comes running—"

"You're scaring me, Blake. Please say *yes.*" Concern colored Hudson's voice.

She smiled to put his fears at ease.

"...but I couldn't hate you," she went on, revealing the deepest truths of her heart. "I think I've loved you all along."

"Then say you'll marry me," he urged. "Say you'll spend the rest of our lives with me, riding my tail, putting me in my place, reminding me I'm not special—"

"You're *kinda* special," she interrupted, eyeing the ring still in his hand.

"Say *yes,* and I'll also be the luckiest man on earth."

From anyone else, the statement would've sounded clingy or cliché. From Hudson — in his deep drawl — the words formed a pledge. A promise. Not a compromise...because they both wanted the same thing: a life together, forever.

"Okay."

"Okay? As in *yes* — you'll marry me? And be careful here. Once you say it, I'll never let you take it back."

"Yes," she laughed over tears of joy. "I'd love to be the one tasked with keeping you humble. It'll be a never-ending assignment. Just like my love: unconditional and everlasting."

Hudson slid the glorious band onto Blake's hand. A perfect fit. The perfect present.

For Christmas, and forever…a life together, a legacy to build, and a love for all time.

————

*Christmas isn't a season.*
*It's a feeling.*
*Eden Ferber*

————

he End.

But not for long. Please enjoy this sneak peek into Book 6…

## ISLA

*I think too many obituaries
have been written about me.*
**Smriti Irani**

*Thursday, February 18, 2021*

### Seamstress Found Dead in Her Boot
### Unknown Woman Dies, Cause Also Unknown
### Braemar Lass Has Threaded Her Last Needle

Huddled in hiding, Isla Scott imagined obituary headlines in *The Scotsman*. Trying to guess the announcement of her seemingly impending death depressed Isla a smidgen less than considering the irreparable damage done to her dress. The vintage shirtdress, a brilliant and bold golden chrysanthemum color and made of divine silk, had been an indulgent splurge, but one she'd simply *had to have* when she'd spotted the rare find at an estate sale on her way to London the day before. The right shoulder seam hadn't just split; the delicate fabric had been shredded in her frantic escape. The left sleeve's wide turned cuff was holding on by a thread. And grease smeared across the once-beautiful fabric from Isla's climb through the lowered passthrough section of the backseat to get into the trunk of her car.

Even worse than the ruined dress, her very favorite stiletto pumps — a retro-style Mary Jane in "Cutie Pie" red and fabulously reminiscent of pinup girls from the 1940s and 50s — had lost an entire heel. The whole *boggin* thing!

*To think, this is how I'll look when they discover my body.* Nàr— *What disgrace.*


The tragic thought put Isla to sleep.

She awoke to the noise of car engines idling and going silent, doors closing, and people chattering. She blinked a few times to clear her foggy mind. The pitch-dark space in which she lay curled like a ball confirmed she'd not yet been rescued, but she'd not yet died either, so that provided some promise.

*It must be morn.*

Giving the warehouse district employees time to saunter into their various work buildings, Isla waited to move a muscle until the voices and footsteps faded into silence. First, she wiggled her fingers and toes. Then she tested her ability to straighten her limbs. Finally, Isla pushed the backseat back down ever so slightly. She crawled just far enough to peek out the car window and breathed a silent prayer of thanksgiving when no one looked back at her.

Without a moment's hesitation, Isla slid into the driver's seat, started the motor, and drove swiftly from the car park. Darting glances in the mirrors to check if someone followed, she drove out of Hackney as quickly as possible. Weaving through the East End, she plugged in her very-dead cell phone, turned it back on, and managed a quick text:

*- In London. Need help. Possibly being followed. Where should I go to lose them?*

Mere seconds later, the phone rang.

"Sorry, Bren. I didn't want to wake you and M'Kenzee so early," she said in place of *hello*.

Isla's childhood classmate Brennigan Stewart and his wife had been staying with his parents in Braemar, their small Scottish village, for almost a year. In that time, the three had developed a fast friendship. Isla had even established a relationship with M'Kenzee's younger sister, Maree Davenport, over video calls and was both thrilled and honored to be designing and sewing Maree's bridal gown for her upcoming wedding at Isla's family home, a manor house on the castle registry in Scotland that Isla and her two sisters had turned into a stunning venue in the breathtaking Highlands.

In fact, Maree's dress — more specifically the exquisite lace Isla envisioned for Maree's gown — had been the sole purpose for the quick shopping trip to London which had resulted in Isla happening upon an almost-murder and her unintentionally foiling the plans of three would-be assassins, whom she desperately wanted to never see again.

"Where are you?" Brennigan didn't waste time with greetings either, nor did he comment on Isla's wish to not bother the couple. An FBI agent, Bren served and protected first. His sense of duty and loyalty ran deep; he'd have been offended and angry had she *not* turned to him first when in a bind. Isla appreciated that about Bren always, but never more than in that moment.

"I just sent my location. I haven't seen anyone behind me, but I'm not sure. And I definitely don't want to stop and find out."

"I'm sending you an address. It's less than an hour away from where you are now; do you have enough gas?"

"Yes, I filled up yesterday when I arrived. Where am I going?"

"Winfield House in Regent's Park. It's where the US

Ambassador lives. Mikey's there — Agent Vela. Do you remember him from the party?"

Oh, Isla remembered.

The tall, dark, handsome American's close-cropped hair, which matched deep brown eyes, and his strong, athletic frame, which filled out his dark charcoal suit quite nicely, had made quite an impression at Bren and M'Kenzee's belated wedding reception the previous weekend. With a five o'clock shadow of stubble along his chiseled jawline and a quiet, serious demeanor, he'd oozed sexy "secret agent man." He'd been so quiet in fact, that besides a quick nod and a brief hello when they'd been introduced, Bren's friend and coworker hadn't spoken to Isla the entire night. He hadn't made small talk, hadn't cracked a smile, and he certainly hadn't asked her to dance. So, while Michael Vela might've made an appearance or two in Isla's dreams the three nights since the party, she was positive he had no idea she existed.

"Isla, you there? Is everything okay?"

"Yes," she stammered. "Sorry, I'm here. I remember Agent Vela, but he won't know me. And isn't he supposed to be on vacation? I remember someone asking him what stops he'd planned in Europe for the remaining few weeks of his trip. I don't want to get in the way of his holiday."

"You're not in the way. He knows you're headed to Winfield House, and Mikey's happy to help you… I promise. When you get there, British authorities will be waiting; they'll want to talk to you. Once you're finished, Mikey's going to drive you home. I—"

"*Nae*, Bren. I *cannae* let him do that. It's a ten-hour drive with stops for food and petrol."

"Isla, I'm tellin' *ye*, it's *nae bother*. Let Mikey take care of *ye*, for me. *Aig toil?* Please?"

Bren shifting in and out of his Scottish dialect — a sure sign he worried for her safety — did the trick. Isla agreed, and

Bren reassured her once more. Then she said goodbye and merged onto the A107.

Just thirty minutes later, an armed police officer waved her green Audi A6 sedan through security gates and into Regency Park. Once through the property entrance, a shiny, unmarked black police SUV took the lead and escorted Isla down a long entry road. They came to a stop on a circle drive in front of a red brick mansion trimmed in pristine white and adorned with stately pilasters. Before Isla had time to cut the engine and unbuckle her seatbelt, Agent Vela stood at her door. What a sight to behold: the midmorning sun shining like a heavenly beacon behind him, Agent Vela looking into her eyes with intense directness — *Could that be concern?* — as his jaw tensed like a tiger ready to pounce. He gripped the handle, waiting for her to unlock the door…like a conquering hero, or at least the protector she didn't mind admitting she needed just then.

The moment she'd done so, he opened the door and bent to see inside the car. He scanned her from head to toe, taking in her frizzy mass of disheveled hair, her ripped and wrinkled dress, and her missing high heel. Then his eyes reversed their path and studied her once again, but from the tip of her toes to the crown of her head before settling back on her face, where he further examined her. Isla warmed under the inspection, fully aware she looked exactly as she felt — exhausted, bruised, and decidedly worse for the wear — yet unable to squelch the blush. Or the increased rhythm of her racing pulse. Or the sudden constriction of her lungs.

*Och.*

On that thought, she gulped. Loudly. Which pulled Special Agent Michael Vela's attention to her throat, which led his gaze to her lips, which burned with such a tingling sensation, Isla had no choice but to moisten them before biting the bottom one. She detested the nervous habit. She'd trained herself *not* to do it over the years. But in especially tense situations, the ingrained behavior took over.

Agent Vela shifted, crouching like a footballer does for a prematch photo, harnessing adrenaline and energy while appearing calm and controlled on the surface. "Are you okay?" he asked.

Then he knocked her hypothetical socks off... He reached to cup her cheek and said softly, "You had us worried."

His gentle touch — platonic, yet not exactly brotherly — paired with the kind compassion in his voice, proved her undoing. Isla tried to answer *yes*, but her voice broke. She blinked faster, but a tear escaped despite her effort to deny its release. Agent Vela ran his thumb across her skin, wiping away the offending result of her tumultuous ordeal.

"It's okay to cry," he told her with a low, deep voice. "After what you've been through, I'd say you're entitled to an entire breakdown. But if you're up to talking through what happened, there's an entire team of officials in there champing at the bit to get to work finding the guys responsible for it."

Isla nodded her head, and Agent Vela smiled. He *smiled*. She'd never seen him smile. He had a beautiful smile. Albeit not a huge one, but one that resonated in his eyes, one that said, *You've got this.*

The effect of that small expression empowered Isla to keep moving forward. The strength of the hand magically holding hers didn't hurt either.

Agent Vela stepped back from the open door, not dropping Isla's hand, but gently tugging to help her from the car. When she wobbled on her broken shoe, he steadied her. When she walked toward the enormous residence, he placed a hand at her lower back lending support. Throughout the barrage of questions, repeated descriptions, and tiring sketches, he never left her side.

And when it was done, when she'd been excused to rest in

the Garden Room while the team conversed further, when Isla looked up at his dashing face and his fathomless dark eyes to thank Agent Vela for his attention and his kindness, he answered in a way she'd never expected...in a way that set a school of butterflies fluttering through her stomach, a way that made her nerves sizzle.

"Isla," he began, a pledge in his tone. "You're safe now. I'm here, and I'm not going *anywhere.*"

# BOOK 5 PLAYLIST

***Music is a moral law.***
***It gives soul to the universe,***
***wings to the mind, flight to the imagination,***
***and charm and gaiety to life and to everything.***
***Plato***

Enjoy the music that helped inspire the story…

1. God Rest Ye Merry Gentlemen - J. L. Marshall
2. The Christmas Kiss - Cupid Lofi Records
3. You're a Mean One, Mr. Grinch - Thurl Ravenscroft & Boris Karloff
4. I Saw Three Ships - Pentatonic
5. Sleigh Ride - Leroy Anderson and the Iain Sutherland Concert Orchestra
6. Go Tell It On the Mountain - Dolly Parton
7. O Come O Come Emmanuel - Allie Peters
8. Christmas Kiss - Erin O'Donnell
9. Let it be Christmas - Alan Jackson
10. Kiss You This Christmas - Why Don't We

11.  Carol of the Bells - The O'Pears
12.  Silent Night - Missy & Blonde
13.  Baby, It's Cold Outside - Dean Martin
14.  It's Beginning to Look a Lot Like Christmas - Perry Como and the Fontane Sisters with Mitchell Ayres and his orchestra
15.  I Want a Hippopotamus for Christmas - Gayla Peevey
16.  Kiss Me Babe, It's Christmas Time - Owl City
17.  Have Yourself a Merry Little Christmas - Judy Garland
18.  A Kiss to Build a Dream On - Louis Armstrong
19.  A Marshmallow World - Jessi Canning

*Available on Spotify as*
*"Book 5: Undeveloped Love*
*by Virginia'dele Smith"*

# ABOUT THE AUTHOR

Ashli Montgomery is a wife, a momma, and an author whose passion is sharing love stories, books, quilts, yoga, recipes, and all of her favorite things in life. She is quilting to mend the mind by spearheading a community of quilters through Quilt 2 End ALZ, Inc., a 501(c)(3) nonprofit she launched to use her quilting hobby as a platform to advocate for an end to Alzheimer's disease.

Ashli writes wholesome and cozy romance under the pen name Virginia'dele Smith to honor Syble Virginia Tidwell, Adele Gertrude Baylin, and Etta Jean Smith. These three cherished grandmothers were beautiful role models, teaching Ashli to love without judgment and to always put family first. Through Grandma Syble's journals and appetite for books, through Momadele's priceless cards and handwritten letters, and through many, many hours of visiting over fabric at Mema's kitchen island, Ashli also learned to treasure words.

Get to know Ashli by subscribing to her newsletter, *The Gazette*, at AshliMontgomery.com

**Titles by Virginia'dele Smith**

Printed in the USA
CPSIA information can be obtained
at www.ICGtesting.com
LVHW031825281123
765178LV00016B/1094